ANDALUSIA DOGS

By Christian Baines

CHAPTER ONE

"You're not supposed to be here."

Alex ignored the uneasy stares of Joanna and Vicente as he fixed Leo with a stare of his own, one he hoped would pierce the slim lump of flesh this witless, self-styled auteur called a brain. "I know that, Leo. We're supposed to be on stage. Right now. Rehearsing. You're supposed to be gone."

Leo responded with the kind of exaggerated eye roll that could only preface a bald-faced lie. "Maria knows we need more rehearsal time than you do. This is an epic fantasy allegory of our country's endurance under Franco—"

"It's a rehash of *Alice in Wonderland* that has nothing to do with Franco."

"—and we need all the time we can get. Do you think your little one-man, late-night stand-up show needs as much rehearsal time as—"

"That one *woman* is standing right here," Joanna interrupted, her voice laced with cheerful menace. "And it's a bold dance retelling of *Blood Wedding* with a script that would make Lorca proud."

"It's a script that would make Lorca glad he's dead."

"Who cares what you think, Leo?" Vicente growled. "Seriously, man. You've got six rehearsals booked this week, and that's not enough? You've got to cut into our time too?"

"Exactly!" Alex scraped the bar with his fingernails. "You've got six rehearsals on the schedule, we've got two. So, we'd appreciate it if you'd pack your little epic fantasy up for the day and give us the time we've booked."

Leo flicked his head toward the end of the bar. "Why don't you take out the garbage under the bar? It's starting to stink."

"Go fuck a cactus, Leo."

Before Joanna could squeeze Vicente's hand to calm him down, a small woman in a blue, blood-stained doll's dress stuck her head out from the theatre door to check on the commotion. Then came two long, lopsided ears belonging to a March hare, a dusty, oversized hat sported by an equally oversized woman whose beard fell over her ample breasts like a winter shawl, and a White Rabbit mask whose incisors, Alex thought, had missed slicing Alice's throat by inches.

Joanna folded her arms. "Congratulations, Leo. I think this is your biggest audience yet."

Leo scoffed. "I have four scenes to rehearse today."

"Four? Do you?" Alex asked. "Well, that's your bad timing. It's our turn."

A malevolent grin crossed Leo's face. "I'll tell you what. Take the garbage out. Then, one more scene and the theatre's all yours."

"And let you lock us out?" Joanna pushed a long lock of dark hair off her face and put her hands on her hips. "No, thanks."

"Well one of you better settle it before I cancel both your bookings and offer them to the university," Maria, the theatre manager, said from the lobby as she closed her office door. She was five-foot-two and looked old enough to be the Virgin's grandmother. She puffed her cigarette, eyeing the assembled company of two annoyed directors, Joanna, Vicente, a White Rabbit, a March Hare, a Hatter, a caterpillar, a blood-spattered doll holding a stuffed kitten, a man with a Franco moustache drowning in the royal robes of *La Reina Roja*, and two playing card guards who battled the flimsy construction of their costumes to keep their shoulders upright.

"We have the theatre from five until seven. That's all there is to it." Vicente turned to Maria. "I'm right, aren't I?"

Maria shrugged. "Do you think I keep all that business in my head? What I do know is that I can't think a damn with you lot babbling on out here."

"We extended our booking until six," Leo said. "Hey, I'm sorry you weren't told, Alex."

"Who would have told me?" Alex snarled. "Maria?"

"Like hell." Maria slipped behind the bar and poured herself a vermouth. "You kids think I'm your secretary, too? Holy Mother, I swear—"

"I…." Every set of eyes turned to the White Rabbit, who shuffled his feet in front of the theatre's entrance, a script hanging from oversized paws crossed with contrition. "I might have forgotten to tell them."

"You *what?*" hissed Leo. "Seriously? I asked you to do one thing!"

"On top of learning three parts in this play?"

"Isn't that your stage manager's job?" asked Vicente.

As if on cue, João stumbled behind the rabbit, dropping a silver tray that send a cascade of plastic tea cups and saucers clattering to the floor.

"Right," Alex said. "You're not only working your cast half to death, but your crew as well."

"How about I manage my play and you manage yours?" Leo said.

"We would, but someone double-booked our rehearsal time."

"Right." Maria drained her vermouth in one gulp. "That settles that. Leo? Take your zoo and go. I'll see you tomorrow—God help me."

"It's going to take twenty minutes to pull down." João nervously got to his feet, cups and saucers still rattling on their tray.

"Twenty minutes?" asked Alex. "Where'd you set this? The fucking Alhambra?"

Vicente shook his head. "There's no point, man. Our run time's an hour."

"That's not my problem," Leo said, shooting his cast the look of a man on the verge of a burst blood vessel. "Well? What are you waiting for? Twenty minutes, let's go."

Leo ushered the denizens of Wonderland back inside the theatre, except for the White Rabbit, who removed his mask and ears to reveal a contrite expression on a face Alex, in truth, now wanted to see in a very different setting.

"I'm really sorry about that," the rabbit said, holding his mask by the incisors. He reached into the pockets of his clownish pantaloons. After pulling out a prop pocket watch, a wad of used gum, and a half-eaten cookie, he grinned with triumph, retrieving a wrinkled flyer. "Here. When you're done with rehearsal, come see the movie I'm in. I'll put you on the list."

"Movie?" Joanna asked, peering over Alex's shoulder.

"*Pepi, Luci, Bom and Other Girls from the Heap*?" Alex said. "Which one are you playing?"

"Hah, you're funny. I show my cock in it."

"That's pertinent information," said Alex, his nascent attraction growing. "Thanks."

"Maybe I'll see you there? Sorry again for the mix-up." The White Rabbit grinned, catching his rabbit ears in the doorway as he rejoined his cast.

"What do you want to do?" Vicente asked.

Alex spied the bottle Maria had left on the counter. "Drink?"

Without a better idea, the three of them left the theatre with a half-finished bottle of vermouth and a creased invitation to see the White Rabbit's cock.

* * *

'List' was a generous term for the loosely enforced sheet of names held at the Alphaville cinema's entrance. The squat, bearded man running the door barely glanced at it when they arrived, preferring instead to flirt with a robust-looking fellow whose jawline was so sharp, Alex half expected it to slice a chunk off the doorman's Brigitte Bardot wig should the two ever have the misfortune to collide.

"I don't see anyone checking tickets," said Vicente, stepping aside to let two women chase one another through the lobby. One pelted the other with wrapped candies before catching up to her and taking her in a big, sloppy kiss.

"Friends and family night?" Joanna made a face as the chaser popped an unwrapped bonbon into her mouth. She forced a smile, spat the questionable candy into her hand and tossed it in the trash.

"I guess so?" Alex looked back at Bardot, who, having lost his object of flirtation, was now in decidedly grumpier conversation with a different man, tanned, slender and modest of stature, wearing a plaid shirt.

"I'm getting popcorn," Vicente said at last. "Do you want anything?"

"Do you smell popcorn?" asked Joanna. "The Alphaville doesn't serve it."

"What?" Vicente poked his head through the doors to the cinema, wincing at the cacophony of drums, cymbals, and other noises that rose from the rowdy crowd inside. "You're joking."

Alex watched as Bardot got more and more frustrated with Plaid Shirt, who, if Alex could read body language, insisted he was on the list Bardot had been happy to ignore when he'd been making eyes at Jawline, trying to sow the seeds for a good dicking. Alex was about to turn away when Plaid Shirt turned and caught his eye, the edge of his mouth curling with a shy smile. Without thinking, Alex doubled back to the ornate doors. "He's with us."

"Huh?" Bardot grunted, moustache twitching as he looked at the list. "I thought you were three."

"Must be a mistake," said Alex. "The guy who put us on the list isn't good with these things."

This part was true at least. Bardot rolled her eyes, pushed several blonde tresses behind his ear with a plump, hairy hand, and admitted Plaid Shirt.

"Thanks." Plaid Shirt squeezed Alex's arm, then vanished into the cinema.

"You're welcome?" He felt Joanna's hand where the stranger's had just been.

"That," she said, "may be the briefest love affair I've seen."

Alex snorted, trying to clear his head with a shake. "What are you talking about?"

She purred at him while tickling his chin. "Your cluelessness is far too endearing."

"Are you two coming?"

By the time they walked into the theatre, an excited audience had filled most every available seat. At last, Vicente spied three vacant spots on the edge of the fifth row. It wasn't an ideal angle for the screen, but the people-watching more than made up for it. Three or four colourful wigs stood out over the assembled crowd. Their wearers strutted up and down the aisle on oversized heels and masculine legs, tossing grapes into the crowd. Their cries of "Feliz queer nuevo!" made little sense to Alex or those few paying enough attention to catch the grapes. It was high summer, after all.

Spying his frown, Joanna explained. "It's an English pun. Like Feliz año nuevo, but in English, 'year' rhymes with—"

"Hence the grapes. Got it." Alex remembered his first New Year in Madrid and a valiant attempt to stuff all twelve grapes into his mouth for luck before the bells stopped tolling midnight. It had been the first year he'd failed, but it had also been his first year trying to do it with cava being poured down his throat. "Are they English?"

"I don't think so, darling."

Vicente grunted. "So, the theatre won't allow popcorn, but grapes mashed into the carpet are okay?"

Joanna turned to Vicente and squeezed his hand. "Corazon, I love you, but stop sulking."

One of the drag queens rounded the row and dropped into the seat in front of Joanna, who tapped her on the shoulder. "Excuse me, but your wig?"

With a dismissive sniff, the queen lifted the towering follicle construct off her head in one clean movement, revealing a smooth head of dark, slicked-back hair.

Joanna leaned into Vicente. "Amor, I still can't see. Can we change places?"

With a shrug, Vicente changed seats with Joanna and settled into the centre seat behind the drag queen, whose height posed him no challenge. Alex thought he caught a knowing glance from Joanna, but he couldn't be sure. She seemed to be nodding at something over his left shoulder. He turned to see a number of people surrounding a man with a frizzy shock of thick, dark hair who looked to be thanking them through obvious nerves. Just behind him, sat Plaid Shirt, who caught Alex's eye and smiled.

The lights dimmed. The crowd's enthusiasm rose into a deafening thunder of cheers and applause as the man Bardot had been trying to chat up, took the stage. He invited up the man with the frizzy hairdo, introducing him as the director, then a couple of other cast members—not including the White Rabbit—before they ceded the stage to someone called Alaska, who also appeared in the film. She powered through several numbers with a Siouxie Sioux look and a Patti Smith confidence Alex admired.

Onscreen, they later watched Alaska urinate on her co-star and love interest while Carmen Maura—who Alex had seen in several movies and who must have been quite a get for the young director—watched with excitement like she'd found the spring of Lourdes. When they came to the White Rabbit's promised phallic debut, he felt Vicente's fingers brush the edge of his hand. He glanced over to see Joanna leaning against Vicente's chest with his arm wrapped around her. But Vicente's other hand remained next to his. Something in him jolted as Vicente slid a little finger around his and left it there. Vicente grinned at the screen as the camera followed Maura and an emcee played by the director down a line of stiffies. In what the screenplay called a 'General Erection,'

Maura measured the length and girth of each before declaring a winner.

Alex had missed the White Rabbit entirely.

He made a haphazard attempt to follow the rest of the plot; something about a housewife who'd spurned the affections of Alaska's punk-rocker in favour of an abusive… he'd decided early in the film not to overanalyse it. Every so often, he would feel the brush of Vicente's finger against his, and less often, a glance from Plaid Shirt, whose face he would catch across the aisle as the screen filled with light.

As Pepi—Maura—led Bom—Alaska—to a presumably happy ending without the complication of noncommittal, masochistic housewife lovers, the crowd erupted in raucous cheers. Joanna and Vicente leapt to their feet and joined them. Meanwhile, Alex tracked the departure of Plaid Shirt, who looked back with a mischievous smile before disappearing into the lobby.

The director returned to the stage for bows, along with Alaska and the actor who'd played the housewife. After what felt like more than five minutes of applause, the crowd was on the move again, some meandering to the exit half-drunk, others mobbing the director and stars with praise.

"Come on, let's say hello!" Joanna said, nodding at the director and hauling Vicente into the aisle.

"Wait, you know him?" Vicente asked.

"Does that matter?" She turned to Alex. "Are you coming?"

Alex shook his head. The growing crowd around the director was the last thing he felt like dealing with. "Congratulate him for me?"

He watched Joanna and Vicente join the growing throng before following the stragglers out into the warm night. For whatever hellish heat Madrid endured through each of its August days, there was something magical about it after dark—not just because Plaid Shirt now stood there smoking on the pavement, giving Alex a shy smile as he approached.

"Wild movie, huh? The critics will hate it."

"Probably," Alex agreed, refusing his offer of a cigarette. "Do you think the guy who made it cares?"

Plaid Shirt smiled again. "I've his band, so I don't think he does."

"He has a band too?" Alex stepped out of the way of a six-foot five transvestite who tottered by on precarious heels.

Plaid Shirt nodded. "How about you?"

"I don't… Oh, I'm a director too. Theatre, though. Well, I'm trying to be."

"God, another one?" Plaid Shirt blew a puff of smoke out toward the street. His face fell as he turned back to Alex. "I'm sorry, that sounded dismissive. I'm sure you're very good."

Alex flirted with the idea of mining their evening's rehearsal drama for an anecdote, but it seemed a sure way to drive the stranger away. "I'm Alex."

"Jago." The man's grip belied his small frame.

"Like in *Othello*?"

"Oof!"

"I'm sorry. *That* sounded—"

"No, I deserved it." Jago smirked. "Actually, Iago is a form of 'James.' My full name is Jacobo, but please, Jago. Just Jago."

Alex watched Jago stamp out his cigarette. "Sounds like you've had this conversation before."

"I was wondering if I wanted to have it with you, or if you would want to talk with me at all. While I was considering this, out you came like a cuckoo clock. Some would call that fate."

Alex felt what a cliched romance novel might have called butterflies. He called it regretting so much vermouth.

"Was that your boyfriend sitting next to you?" Jago asked.

"Oh. No. Actually he's… My friends have been together almost a year now."

"Ah, the girl? A most handsome couple."

Alex's mind reached for an appropriate follow-up question. Was Jago seeing anyone? Too intrusive. What did Jago do? Too obvious, and what if the poor guy worked at a bank or a café like Alex did when he wasn't being a director? If this had been the movie, it would have been the perfect time for Vicente and Joanna to join them and save Alex from the pregnant silence. Not that Jago couldn't have ended it any time he chose. In fact, Alex was starting to think he'd deliberately chosen not to, until at last he lit another cigarette.

"What play are you doing?" asked Jago. "I'd like to come see it."

"It's umm… an homage to… well, more of a retelling, really… you know Lorca's *Blood Wedding*?"

Jago's eyes darkened, casting Alex a side glance thick with scepticism. "Everyone. Knows. *Blood. Wedding.*"

The response had been so stilted and unreal, Alex was unsure how to respond, until Joanna and Vicente burst through the Alphaville's doors.

"So much fun!" Joanna beamed at Alex. "Didn't you have fun, darling? You should have joined us. Everyone's quite friendly."

"I had fun. It was just stuffy in there. Oh, this is…" Alex turned to the empty space where Jago had been. He looked around for any sign of a plaid shirt, only to see it vanish around the next corner.

*   *   *

"They'll hate it."

"You might be surprised."

"No, they're going to hate it," Vicente insisted, a cigarette wedged between his lips as he emptied the last of the vermouth into two glasses. "They're going to hate it because they're obsessed with this strange pre-Fascist golden age that never existed, like every artist who came out of that age didn't fuck off to Paris or Mexico or stay to be murdered by Franco. *That's* the fantasy they want to see. Not housewives pissing on lesbian punk rockers. Alex? Alex!"

"Eh? Oh!" Alex took the glass from Vicente's hand, watching in silence as Vicente sat down opposite him. "No more ice?"

"No, and you're too drunk to care." Joanna leaned into Vicente's chest as he took a sip of warm vermouth. "So, did you have an actual conversation this time?"

Vicente and Alex frowned at her.

"With that boy who disappeared on you after you got him into the movie."

"Oh, umm…" Alex held up his glass. "You're not having more?"

"There's no more to have. Also, you're dodging the question. Did you talk to that boy or not?"

"I did. We did. Talk, that is, with Jago."

"What?"

"His name. His name's Jago."

"I heard you. *Like Othello?*" Vicente put out his cigarette in a brown glass ashtray on the table.

"No, *E-yay-go*, not *Ee-ah-go*. Look, it doesn't matter."

"And what did you and Jago talk about?"

A cool pre-dawn breeze from the open window of their apartment stirred Alex from his exhaustion. In truth, he'd paid less attention to Jago's words than to his tone, his lips, and the playful cadence of his voice, at least until the deadly seriousness of that last statement.

Everyone. Knows. Blood. Wedding. Man, Alex thought, chill out.

"The movie," he murmured at last. "He liked it."

Joanna winced as the first rays of dawn warmed the windows. "If you say so. I'm going to bed."

Vicente caught her hand as she rose from the couch. "I'll be there soon."

"Nonsense. You're wired," she said, kissing him on the cheek. She reached a playful hand inside his shirt to brush his chest, then turned to Alex. "Stay as long as you like, darling. Our couch is yours."

"Thanks," Alex lifted his glass again, as if Joanna had not made this exact offer after a dozen drunken nights before. She was gone before he could say goodnight.

Vicente undid another button on his shirt and slumped further into the couch. "We never go out dancing anymore."

"Sorry?"

"I just mean…" Vicente leaned forward, fingers cradling the glass until he downed the last of his vermouth and set it down on the stained coffee table.

Alex always thought it was curious Vicente and Joanna could afford a one-bedroom apartment with its own bathroom and kitchen this close to Gran Via, while luxuries like ice, spare liquor and well-kept furniture seemed to elude them. Not that he could criticise from his tiny studio, where on a clear night, one could hear the sound of scooters carrying customers in need of a fix roaring into Plaza de Chueca, until the disco beats from Black and White drowned them out.

Alex started as Vicente patted the couch where Joanna had been. His face darkened.

"Sorry," they both said at once. Vicente grinned as Alex accepted his invitation, not just to the opposite couch, but to lay his head in Vicente's lap, as they'd done countless times before.

Vicente brushed a wayward lock of Alex's fringe off his face. "You're worried about the play?"

Alex gave as close to a shrug as he was able, lying down. "I suppose? We don't have long."

"We've got long enough. Relax. You're good at this, you know?"

"Do *you* know?" Alex laughed. "It's my first play."

"Shhhh. Don't wake Joanna."

"Joanna never wakes up."

This much was true. Once Joanna crashed in the early hours, there would be no return until sunset. In fact, Alex seldom remembered seeing her in daylight, and on the two occasions he had, she'd dressed top to toe in black like a mourning widow during Holy Week.

"So, what did you think of this guy?" Vicente said, casually draping an arm over Alex's chest. "I'm exercising ex-boyfriend privilege here. Tell me everything."

Alex wrapped both hands around Vicente's forearm, pushing his fingers through the blanket of light hairs that covered it. The scent of Vicente's cigarette burned his nose. "How do you want me to answer that? We had one conversation. He left. I don't think he likes me much."

Only Vicente could squeeze his shoulder like that and not make it feel patronising.

"What?" Alex laughed. "I'm not invested."

"I know that, man. I just… you're still a catch, that's all."

"Still?" Alex turned his shoulders, reaching up to stroke his fingertips against the uneven hairs of Vicente's struggling beard. He'd never known a man to be quite so hairy below the neck, only to have his face denied. In the few short months they'd dated, Alex had found it endearing. He closed his eyes, letting his touch slip down Vicente's throat to the trimmed hairs of his chest.

"I'm not growing it out."

Alex laughed. "That's not what I was—"

"Liar. You absolutely were thinking that."

Alex shifted his weight again, resting his cheek against Vicente's body, the scent of tobacco, vermouth, and the curious citrus soap he'd used as long as Alex had known him, all too familiar. "We're not wasting our time, are we?"

Vicente shrugged, giving Alex's hand a squeeze. "I don't regret what we're doing, if that's what you mean."

He eased himself off Vicente's lap and kissed his cheek. "I should go."

"Are you sure, man? The couch is yours if you want it."

Alex smiled, rehearsing the lie in his head. "Yeah, I'm sure."

CHAPTER TWO

If spending the night with Vicente and Joanna held one distinct advantage, it was access to a private bathroom. Alex tapped his foot as he tried to go over the revisions he'd made to the script two days prior, but Joanna might as well have recited them in Basque for all the sense they made to him.

It had been pushing six in the morning by the time he'd stripped off his clothes and tumbled into his single bed, and even then, sleep had evaded him until eight. Whether this was the nascent sunlight, the noise from the street, or the image of Jago haunting his thoughts—probably all three—didn't much matter. He'd be late for an eleven o'clock shift if he didn't move his ass, and while it wouldn't be the first time he'd gone in smelling like punk rock, vermouth, and Vicente, he was sure it wouldn't endear him to Victoria.

He crossed the hall and hammered on the bathroom door again.

"Just a minute."

"You said that ten minutes ago."

Hearing the shower at last, Alex returned to his room in search of breakfast. He knew complaining was gauche for a boy who'd grown up in the country with no running water or electricity, but hadn't Madrid promised him better for the fortune it cost him to stay here? Joanna had sworn Barcelona was worse, but Alex wasn't convinced.

Taking a piece of bread from its box on his side table, he smeared a spoonful of tomato on it and took a bite. He gagged, gulping it down quickly like a pelican before lifting the jar to his nose, recoiling at the sight of mould growing in the jar. Well, fucking great. He could already hear his mother's lecture to buy his tomatoes fresh each day, as if she was going to give him the money to pay for them. He wondered how many more free meals he could charm out of Victoria before she refused.

Hearing the bathroom door open, he grabbed his towel, narrowly missing a collision with the bald-headed fellow from Zaragoza. Alex had tried to avoid him ever since he'd made a drunken pass at Alex at Black and White. He'd used up most of the hot water, but it didn't much bother Alex in the summer heat. He stuck out his tongue, as if he could wash the bitter taste of rotten tomato from it along with the smell of the night's entertainment. The smell of Vicente. He lifted his hands to his face. No, that wasn't Vicente. Vicente's smell, he knew all too well. Joanna? No, it was a masculine scent, but not one he recognised… at first. He allowed the water to sloosh down his back until a knock at the bathroom door startled him.

"Just a minute," he called.

Now his tired mind was playing tricks, convincing him that his hands smelled like Jago.

* * *

"Good morning, Senor Vargas."

"Good morning, Lucia," Alex said, again hoping his shirt wouldn't crumple in his knapsack as he descended the last of the stairs to the building's sparse entryway. "Having a good day?"

Lucia, who kept an eagle-eyed watch over their boarding house, barely looked up from her copy of *El Pais*. "Is it? These Basque hardliners complain louder every day. Something terrible will come of it if the government doesn't let them go, I promise you."

Alex grimaced, keeping his expression neutral as possible, even though she wasn't looking at him. This wasn't a topic he'd raised with Joanna, and he certainly wasn't about to get into it with a seventy-six-year-old widow.

"But…" She looked up from her paper, folding it neatly as she stood. "It is not all bad. The Americans are returning *Guernica*."

"Oh, that's wonderful." Alex decided against pointing out that the Americans had been returning *Guernica* at least three or four times before in the year he'd called this place home. But Lucia had been just as excited each time over the painting's return, and he hadn't the heart to dim her fire. "I'd love to chat, but Victoria hates it when I'm late."

She waved off his anxiety with a plump hand. "Wait, just one second."

He indulged her, shifting nervously until she returned with a small paper bag.

"She will hate it less if you bring her some of these, *after* you take your share, of course."

Alex inspected the contents. A dozen cookies coated in sugar, and at the bottom of the bag, a small, tightly wrapped package he knew would contain three or four joints.

"Lucia, I can't take these to work."

The old woman pouted indignantly. "What grumpy bitch would begrudge you a few cookies?"

He grinned at her conspiratorially, tucking the bag deep into his knapsack. Bidding him good day, Lucia withdrew to the tiny ground floor apartment she occupied which doubled as her office, muttering something about him not running into or sucking off any police officers along the way. Alex couldn't hear her clearly, but he was sure it was the latter. Hmph. That had only been once. In the stairwell. And she *had* allowed them to finish on the condition they not leave a mess.

The walk from his apartment through Chueca to the Plaza Mayor would take a brisk twenty minutes if the Puerta del Sol wasn't packed. That was no sure thing. Even with classes in summer recess, few of the young, energetic students who'd flocked from around the country to make their contribution to—or take their bite from—Madrid's free hedonism wanted to return to the sleepy church bells, gossip-hunting glares, and dead-after-dark piety of their home towns. On the city's biggest public square, that meant one thing… protests.

Red banners, Basque flags, and signs calling for independence, protesting the steps the new government had taken to try and retain Joanna's home province, flooded the square, waving and turning over in the late morning sun like waves turned red by a volcanic sunset. Alex shook off the romantic metaphor and stuffed Lucia's cookies into the side pocket of his bag. He'd need them for the inevitable grovelling.

Keeping to the edge of the square, he tried to circumvent the crowd. But as he pushed nearer the demonstration's ringleaders, who'd taken up position with speakers and bullhorns on the square's western edge, the crowd swelled to its edges, spilling into the streets that fed it. He barely dodged another banner as its owner climbed the steps from the metro. With a quick apology, they too disappeared into the fray. Alex swallowed his nerves as the bodies of eager protesters, stripped down in the summer sun and painted with reds and greens, including one that resembled Jesus, bounced off him. He grimaced at the smear of green paint on his sleeve, grateful he'd kept his clean shirt in his knapsack as he pulled it tighter against his body.

Another shove, unintentional as it was, sent him stumbling forward. If he could just make it… no. He'd never seen a protest this size, not even on the Puerta del Sol. How many of the assembled crowd were invested in Basque independence and how many were invested in something to do on a Saturday, he couldn't tell. But he could feel his breath quicken as the heat of so many bodies caged him, amplified by the hateful ball of hot gas slowly cooking him from above in his black t-shirt. He cried out as the momentum of the crowd caught him once more, until at last, a street sign indicating Calle de Preciados promised him freedom.

He didn't wait for a second invitation, weaving his way between protestors until he at last broke free of the stragglers coming down from Gran Via. Darting left again, he took a second to catch his breath on Calle de Tetuan. This was fine. It wasn't the first time he'd avoided a protest on the square. He checked his watch, tummy still rumbling. A few months ago, he would have had time to stop at San Ginés for some breakfast, but a steadily increasing number of English tourists had made that a dicey proposition. To hell with it. Victoria's churros would do.

Another left led him toward Calle de Arenal, but the regular hum of the city had quieted, leaving in its place low voices and the clip-clopping of hoofs. He glanced behind him, eyes widening to see a line of mounted police keeping a steady pace behind, black uniforms and helmets looming over their steeds like battlements.

He moved to quicken his step, then hesitated, acutely aware of eight pairs of eyes—not counting the horses—watching him. As he crossed Calle de Arenal, and the street narrowed approaching Calle Mayor, they neither hastened nor broke off their steady rhythm. Would it be smarter to let them pass? Or would that draw just enough attention to invite a quick search that would quickly find the weed buried under the cookies in his bag? They weren't here for him. But under the Fascists, the police had been predictably brutal; something to be avoided at any cost. Things were less predictable now, even in Madrid. Not all of them wanted to trade blow jobs in a stairwell. But if he could just get across Calle Mayor…

He could no longer ignore the shouts of the crowd as it funnelled slowly from the square into the street, any more than he could ignore the sound of hooves behind him. By the time he saw Basque Jesus, leading the protest in all his red and green painted non-finery spy the line of police closing at his left, facing them with shields and batons at the ready, Alex knew it was too late to run.

As the mounted cops closed off any chance of escape, Alex retreated into the relative safety of a café's shuttered doorway. Seconds ticked by until the scene reached its inevitable combustion. The protestors charged first, not with violence, but taunting the steel-faced officers with the same slogans Alex had heard in the del Sol. They stopped just as abruptly, and for a moment, he felt himself relax, some naïve corner of his brain hoping this would be the sum of strife on Calle Mayor that morning.

Without warning, the crowd charged. The police responded in kind. Horses blocked off his retreat. A flaming bottle sailed over Basque Jesus's head before exploding at the feet of the cops. It was the perfect starting gun, as if Satan himself had lifted the gates of hell.

As more people swelled into the intersection, Alex resisted the tidal crowd, trying to put some distance between him and the horses, only to catch an elbow to the face. From the corner of his eye, he saw several protesters, including Basque Jesus, go down, felled by the unsanctimonious blow of a baton. His creative mind had just enough time to wonder what the deceased dictator's cronies in the church would have thought before something clocked him hard across the cheek, toppling him into the street. Curling his body into a foetal ball, Alex tried to protect his head, as one stray kick and footstep landed after another, each no more malicious than the last, but stinging with the bruise of a fight that wasn't his.

"*Come on!*"

A pair of firm hands gripped his underarms and hoisted him to his feet. The taste of blood filled his mouth, the shouts of the crowd filled his ears, and an acrid mingling of blood, horses, summer sweat and rage pricked his nostrils, any trace of the peaceful demonstration that had filled the square now caught alight on the leftover embers of some Fascist bootlickers eager to crack some leftie heads.

With an arm draped across his Samaritan's shoulders, Alex at last recognised him.

"We have to stop meeting like…" He abandoned the attempt to be funny.

Jago shot him a sly smirk. "Just keep moving."

They didn't stop until they were well away from the crowd, narrowly dodging another dozen police who'd been waiting in the Plaza Mayor. Alex took a moment to catch his breath in one of the side streets, startling a cat from its investigation of breakfast's leftovers.

"Let me see you." Jago examined his face with cold passivity. "I think you're okay. Can you walk? I can't carry you."

He backed away as Alex coughed. When no blood came up, he took it as a good sign. "I'm fine, thanks. Lucky you were there."

"I don't envy your luck today, my friend. That could have been much worse for you." Jago shook his head as more cops paused at the end of the alley. They looked straight at the boys for a moment, then kept running toward the sound of the angry crowd as it grew louder.

"Yes, yes, I know. Like I said, thank you. Where... I need to..." He eased himself off the wall and staggered forward a couple of steps until Jago caught him again.

"Woah, where are you going?"

"Work." Alex held up the miraculously unscathed satchel. "I'm okay, really. It's just on the other side of the plaza. I just need—"

"You need rest. A few inches to the right and that cop would have stomped your head in." Jago squeezed his shoulder, belying his stern expression. "I think that deserves a sick day."

"Don't be stupid. I'll just..." A wave of nausea collapsed him against the wall once more. "I'll just tell Victoria I'm sick."

"Tell her the truth. She'll understand. Hell, *I'll* call her. You take it slow."

"You have a phone?"

"In my apartment."

Alex looked up at Jago with a mischievous grin. "Now who needs to take things slow?"

Jago raised an eyebrow. "Another joke?"

"You tell me."

"Come on." Jago took Alex on his shoulders again. "Your sense of humour sucks when you're sick."

* * *

Sleep eluded Alex for the better part of an hour before he at last settled for dozing. He sank his head into the admittedly comfy pillows of Jago's single bed. On the fourth floor, the apartment caught a nice breeze from over the Retiro, and it was only now, caught in the sun's early afternoon barrage that he'd felt stifled by the heat. The hands on the clock next to the bed hadn't moved since his arrival, giving Alex the distinct sense his host and nurse wasn't overly concerned with simple concepts like work and time. Not that he knew anything about his host.

Hell, coming back to Jago's apartment had probably been a terrible idea. But his knapsack remained slung over the handle of the small wardrobe, right where he'd left it. Likewise, his keys and wallet, slim as it was, still sat in his left pocket. Only his belt was… no, there it was with his bag, right where Jago had left it before excusing himself to run the errands interrupted by Alex's rescue.

These details returned to him while he was trying to sit up, as if the very act of lying down had surrendered them. He'd read once dreams were mere memories or fears of the future, masquerading as the present. But he hadn't dozed off, at least not completely. On the way to the flat, he'd pointed out Yolande's bakery, where he and Vicente had enjoyed cheap but filling churros for breakfast every morning until the Plaza Mayor's growing popularity with tourists had priced them out. Jago's only response had been a tender but silent smile.

Yet, he couldn't remember Jago putting him to bed. He was about to call him, but instead looked around the room one last time. Odd. Most rooming houses or even apartments featured at least some sort of iconography. A crucifix, or an image of the Virgin… hell, anything, just for show. He'd hooked up with men whose depravities had played out—with him—under the watchful gaze of Christ himself. But in Jago's room? Nothing.

He cried out as a loud bang came from the open window, followed by the syncopated flap of stunned wings as a pigeon staggered a moment on the roof outside, then tumbled over it. Alex got up to inspect the aftermath. The poor thing's broken body was now no more than a grey lump on the red tiled roof of the neighbouring low-rise, something to be washed away by the next rain shower, whenever that would come. At least it wasn't close enough to stink up the apartment in the heat.

"Alex?"

He started again, seeing Jago in the doorway holding a bottle of red wine and two glasses when he turned. "Jesus!"

"No Jesus here," Jago answered with a satisfied smile.

"I noticed."

Jago gently placed the wine down on the bedside table and shut the door behind him. "I'm sorry I startled you. You're feeling better?"

"Better than someone, that's for sure." He nodded to the ill-fated bird.

Jago grimaced as he inspected the carnage. "Not the first time. I don't really know why. I suppose I should paint something on the window. Or perhaps they are simply tired of life, so... *boom*! Into the window. Lemmings in bird form."

"Lemmings?" Alex toyed with the idea of dispelling his perception of the animal's suicidal ways but decided against it. "Does this happen often?"

"Just this summer. Perhaps the heat makes them crazy? I really don't know. Come, sit." Jago poured a glass of wine. "Have you tried Bobal? Valencia's liquid treasure."

"No, I don't think I have. Is that where you're from?"

Jago handed Alex the glass and poured another. "Just one for you. Nurse's orders."

"Yes, sir."

"Hah!" Jago set the bottle down with a thump. "Would that turn you on? A masochist, like Luci in the movie? Perhaps I should piss on you?"

"You're kidding?"

"Of course I'm kidding. *Salud.*"

They lifted their glasses high and drank together. The wine didn't disappoint, though what Alex wasn't sure what he'd been expecting. Bobal? Rioja? Merlot? Wine was wine to him, and it usually came watered down with a lot of ice and fruit.

"That's delicious," he said, mostly out of politeness.

"Damn. I thought I was unloading the cheap stuff on you."

Alex furrowed his brow.

"Still joking."

"Ah."

For all Jago's jokes, his dark brown eyes radiated an unspoken kindness Alex couldn't ignore. "Thank you," he said. "I mean, you really didn't have to do this."

"I was not going to just leave you there on the street. You're not some bird that flew into a window."

"No, but…" Alex wondered how many others had been hurt during the protest. How bad had it gotten? He'd read horror stories of protestors being denied treatment at hospitals or dumped in ditches by the police, and there was no telling if these were true or holdovers from the Franco years. "I'm okay, I think?"

Jago crossed to the window sill and, setting his wine down, lit a cigarette, blowing smoke gingerly into the fresh air. "I think so. I'm not trained, if that's what you're asking. But you were lucid enough as we were walking here. Nothing broken, as far as I can tell. Do you feel okay? No nausea? No pain?"

Alex nodded. In fact, he felt better than okay. Perhaps it was the wine.

"I don't trust hospitals," Jago continued. "My mother in all her life only went inside one. She never came out again."

"I'm sorry to hear that. Can I ask, when did she pass?"

"I did not say she died." Jago blew another long stream of smoke and stubbed out his cigarette, seemingly bored with it. "But without the mind… Anyway, there are benefits to being alone, just as there are benefits to making new friends."

They lifted their glasses again, though it seemed to Alex a macabre sort of toast.

"Andalusia," Jago continued.

"I'm sorry, what?"

"You asked, in your own roundabout way, where I was from? Andalusia. And now, I'm here."

"Nobody in Madrid is from Madrid. Not these days."

"I promise you, that's not true." Jago straightened his shirt, then poured them each more wine. "The *gatos*—that's what they call themselves, the true Madrileños—are still around, and they are quite pleased to let you know it."

The observation made Alex wonder how few true Madrileños he knew. "I thought you said *one* glass of wine?"

"It is a very small glass. You think I'm made of money?" Jago defused this question with another smile as he refreshed Alex's glass.

"Okay. What do you do, then?"

Jago sighed as if the question annoyed him. "Work? The great failing of the *gatos*. Everyone wants to talk about what you do for work, not just in Madrid, but in every big city, everywhere. As if your most interesting feature were what fattened your bank account."

"Not everyone is like that."

"You mean people like you? Like us?" Jago put a hand on Alex's shoulder, and for the first time, Alex was struck by the warmth of his touch. "No, thank the gods. Some music?"

Alex watched Jago pluck a record from a small shelf under what he now realised was a record player, and slide it from its sleeve. He recognised the monochrome image of the American woman pouting at him from between the stern faces of two men from Vicente's collection. "Blondie?"

"I hope you like them?" Jago placed the needle down with a grin, letting the first pulsing drumbeats fill the tiny room. Dreaming, indeed. "I try to buy local music, but until Alaska puts something on a record... I mean, you seemed to like her? Alaska, I mean."

Alex hadn't been conscious of dancing along or even showing much enthusiasm when the punk group had taken the stage. Maybe he had. He seldom had money to buy records. He mostly knew Alaska by reputation and gigs he'd caught here and there. He only vaguely recognised the Blondie song, even as he involuntarily tapped his foot. He stilled it as soon as he noticed.

Jago nodded at his foot. "Are you hurt?"

"No. I just felt silly, I guess."

"Why?" Jago sat down on the bed beside him. "It's a good song, and you're an artist. Music is part of your soul. Music that you love. Music that you hear so much you never want to hear it again. Punk rock. Disco. Your grandmother's favourite folk songs."

"Just no flamenco, okay?" Alex added, feeling noticeably better.

Jago's gaze shifted, as if he were scrutinising his guest, though his smile never wavered. "Perhaps if the ban had stayed, you'd get your wish?"

Alex's smile drained from his face. "I'm sorry. I didn't mean... You're not Roma, are you?"

Jago let out a sharp, piercing laugh, covering his face as he flopped down on the bed. "No, no, it's all right, really. I'd just rather talk about the music we love. Anything we love."

Alex shrugged, relaxing again. "Speaking of music you hear so much you never want to hear it again? Franco hadn't been dead two hours when my abuela started clapping and tapping away. We just stared at her. We all knew about her heritage, but she'd never talked about it. She just got on with life. Then, suddenly, it came out in one big dancing rush. It was the strangest, most beautiful thing I'd ever seen. She didn't even keep in time. Just kept tapping and clapping, singing, if you could call it that, but she didn't care. I guess that's what thirty years out of practice will do to you."

"I'd think that would give you reason to love flamenco, yes?"

"Right, except she didn't stop until she died. Almost every day for three years, like a ritual. Until one day it was quiet. Okay, one day wasn't so strange. Then came another. Six days of quiet. Then we said goodbye."

No trace of the harshness that had crossed Jago's face moments earlier remained. He just stared at Alex with kind eyes, the back of his fingers brushing Alex's knee, not daring to patronise him by patting it. "You may not agree, but that's actually a lovely reason for not wanting to hear it. Thank you for sharing that memory with me."

Alex swallowed, unable to hide his awkwardness. The next song on the record, something in English about an armoured car, wasn't helping. "I feel like I've killed the mood."

"What mood?"

"Oh. Sorry, I thought…" Just when he'd thought nothing could make this more awkward, Jago leaned in, slowly, carefully, with tender consideration as if it were Alex's first time. Jago's kiss was sweet with wine, but under that, Alex tasted a power that excited him. A rich invitation to be himself, to tap along with whatever damn song he liked, and perhaps even jump up singing, dancing, tapping and clapping just as his abuela had.

Jago withdrew with a satisfied look, at last putting his hand on Alex's leg. "I'm glad you wanted that too. Otherwise, I would have been the one killing the mood."

"How did you know I—"

"I didn't. I took a risk." Jago stood, draining the last of his wine. "Though not one as big walking through a potentially violent protest on your way to work. Try to sleep. If you need anything, call out."

"Thanks," Alex murmured, though Jago was already gone. Try to sleep? The suggestion made him smile as he turned off the record player.

The sounds of the street floated into the room on another warm gust of breeze. Despite his protestations that Alex should have only one, Jago had left the bottle. Screw it. Not feeling the pull of sleep, he poured himself a little more wine and sat on the window sill, where the sun warmed his face. It was in this moment of complete calm that something in his gut seized. He couldn't remember calling Victoria. Even on her most easy-going days, his boss wasn't a fan of 'no call, no show.' Did Jago even have a phone? Yes, he'd said as much, hadn't he?

Alex opened his mouth to call out when he heard a latch lifting below. A window swung open, and out onto the roof of the neighbouring building popped Jago. Alex watched in silence as he skittered across the roof, agile as a cat until he reached the dead pigeon. He unfolded a large piece of newspaper from his pocket and wrapped it around the broken body, cradling it with care.

Jago looked up, saw Alex watching, and smiled. "If I leave them, we get rats."

Rats? Alex took another sip of his wine as he watched Jago return to the window, nimble as he'd been before. The wine tasted bitter compared to before, either from the heat or the sight of Jago scooping up the unfortunate bird. He couldn't imagine stray cats ignoring such a prize for very long, and even so, why hadn't Jago just tossed it to the street?

He drained the last of his wine, quietly stunned he'd not only finished it but wanted more. Would it be rude? No, Jago had presumably left him the bottle for that very purpose, and he felt fine. Better than fine. Whatever Jago had done for him had worked a treat. In that case, he reasoned, it was probably better to leave explaining things to Victoria and begging forgiveness until tomorrow. Right now, he looked more like a man enjoying wine in bed than one recovering from an injury.

He poured himself the last of the bottle before noticing the book Jago had discreetly left next to it. *Blood Wedding and Other Works.*

Perhaps some inspiration? read a small note in red ink tucked into the pages.

Alex smiled, stacked another pillow onto the pile and let it envelop him. He picked up the familiar text and thumbed through, barely noticing the rapid descent of sleep until it overtook him.

*　　*　　*

Alex woke with a start, warm air filling his nostrils as he closed his fingers around the hard cover of the book. He could see the silhouette of an almost full glass of red wine beside a lamp on the table beside him. The room's only natural light now came from the reflection of the moon. He gripped the book as an awful thought hit him. Had he missed a rehearsal? Skipping work was one thing, but he couldn't leave Vicente and Joanna in the… No, no, rehearsal had been yesterday. Right. Leo and his Alice in Fucking Wonderland.

He reached for the light switch beside his bed, bumping the empty wine bottle, which landed on the floor with a sharp thud before rolling away. He shifted the near full glass of wine away from the edge of the table.

His senses returning to him at last, Alex thumbed through the book to his favourite part, the Bride's rejection of the gifted orange blossoms. He'd marked it with Jago's note. There was no part of the play he didn't have memorised, of course. Rumours flew that Saura was making a film version. It seemed weirdly appropriate, given that for their second date, Vicente had taken him to see *Ana and the Wolves*, claiming it to be his favourite film. One of Vicente's most endearing qualities was that he had a new favourite film every four to six months. It would come as no surprise to Alex if in a few weeks, Vicente was extolling the virtues of *Pepi, Luci, Bom*.

Alex cradled the handwritten note in his fingers. He'd read that some cultures reserved red ink for writing the names of the dead. He hoped this didn't bode ill for his inspiration. Still, Jago had already gone above and beyond, looking after him. The wine and the book, with such a personal note had been downright sweet.

He got to his feet, slipped on his clothes, picked up his glass of wine, and went in search of his host. He declined to intrude on an empty bedroom he took to be Jago's, which left only a small water closet with a wash basin and the upper banister of an iron spiral staircase, which led down to a well-lit living area.

To say that this was where Jago had concentrated his decorating would have been understating it. Blue walls surrounded him, accented with black shadowy silhouettes sporting forked tails and gnashing sharp teeth. A bright orange couch offered a tenuous link to the 70s while three cushions sheathed in leopard print added a touch of kitsch. The walls of the kitchen were bright red, matching a delightfully audacious kettle and toaster. His host had a penchant for pot plants, which threw splashes of green around the room and almost obscured an ornate, bejewelled peacock that wouldn't have looked out of place on an Argento film.

He paused a moment. No, it was the *exact* prop he'd seen in an Argento film. He half expected to find a personal note to Jago engraved underneath.

A record played in the corner. Not Alaska. Not Blondie. A blues singer from the American South, whose sensuality smoothed the pops and crackling of the vinyl as it gave up its contents to the needle with a quiet hiss. A large black crow that was either stuffed or the most lifelike model Alex had ever seen, watched over it. No, not a crow. A raven.

"Jago?" He coughed as the heat stifled his call. He opened one of the windows. The night air might have been warm, but it was moving. He fetched a glass from the kitchen cupboard, filled it from the tap and downed it, then filled himself another. At least the water was cold. The red walls of the kitchen seemed more suited to the daemons that covered the blue walls of the living room—cast out of Heaven? A cute, if unlikely theme for home décor.

His gaze fell on a large crack in the wall that ran… No, not a crack. A door sat ajar, beckoning him with warm, dim light.

Alex's jaw near fell from its joint. If the living room walls had been the daemon's fall, then this small chamber was their place of bacchanal. A cluster of candles on Jago's desk was the room's only light source, but what artefacts their flickering light found. A figurine made from straw hung on the wall next to a large tapestry divided into four quarters, all covered in geometric symbols beyond his recognition. The underside of a swooping owl reflected more light onto a shelf of ornate books propped up by a skull decorated with gilt paint lines intercut by rusty stains. Another raven stood beside it with its beak open as if telling the grinning death's head a story, and hanging from one of the skull's eye sockets was a thread of black and red beads, which the flickering candlelight gave the appearance of a snake's tail.

He had just made out a wall of photos on the other side of the room when Jago, still seated at his desk, turned to face him, eyes wide like a man possessed, dark fingers white with pressure as he dug them into the back of his chair, looking at Alex like he meant to tear his skin off. On the desk, Alex at last saw the corpse of the broken bird, pinned down by long needles.

"What are you doing in here?"

Words failed him. He could barely look Jago in the eye, much less conjure an excuse that gave him the right to poke about the home of a man who'd shown him only kindness. But he hadn't been expecting…whatever this was.

"Get out!" Jago barked like an attack dog eager to strike. "Get out! I won't tell you again!"

He didn't need to. Alex threw the hidden door shut behind him. He rushed to the mercifully conspicuous front door and hurriedly worked the locks, barely remembering to grab his shoes. He was halfway down the stairs before he heard it slam shut above, and almost to the bottom before he caught enough presence of mind to check that he had his wallet and keys. Jago had left them in his pants pockets, thank God.

But wow. Just… wow.

*   *   *

When a gin and tonic at Black and White failed to steady his nerves, Alex ordered another, then a third, and then—

"Easy," the bartender said quietly, a smile assuring Alex there'd be no further judgement.

Judgement be damned. He needed calm. True, the pulsing disco beats of Blondie were hardly calming. Debbie Harry really had it in for him tonight. He stared into his drink, letting the hypnotic refrain about someone's beautiful hair wash through him. At least it wasn't Donna Summer… again.

Get out. Jago had screamed the words. They'd stung in the moment. Now, they haunted him. *I won't tell you again!*

Good Samaritan or not, he wasn't about to give Jago that opportunity.

"You shouldn't drink so much too quickly."

The voice had come from the end of the bar to his left, where a stranger with close-cut dark hair, full lips and enticing brown eyes clutched a beer. The man's top barely contained his muscular chest. Any sleeves that might once have been attached hadn't stood a hope against those arms.

"Thanks." Alex turned to watch the dance floor. The last thing he needed was mothering from Sister Maria of the Immaculate Pecs. He distracted himself by watching a boy in a leather cap, matching lace-up vest and a floral jacket, whose pace picked up as the music blended over to an Italo Disco song Alex recognised but couldn't name. The boy's thick black eyeliner had started running with sweat, though if he cared, he wasn't showing it. He just lifted his arms high above his head, the vest riding up to reveal a furry belly that belied his boyish face. Perhaps it was just the makeup, but he was hairy as Vicente. Alex bit his bottom lip as the boy caught him looking, scowled, and spun away from him in time to the music.

Had he been that obvious? Maybe, suggested the tightening of his trousers. He raised his drink to his lips and downed it with a swish of ice. Sister Maria Pecs walked by, offering him another mischievous look. Alex allowed himself to watch him disappear into the bathroom, biting his bottom lip again. Not his usual type, yet at the same time, everybody's type. Hell, sex was about the last thing on his mind. As hard as his dick wanted to be in the moment, all his mind could hear was Jago's rage. *Get out! I won't tell you again.*

He tried to catch the eye of the bartender, who was already serving another customer. Maybe after one more drink he could hit the dance floor with fewer cares than the boy in the mismatched leather and florals.

He started bopping his head as a Radio Futura song coxed another wave of guys onto the floor, along with Sister Maria Pecs.

"You feeling okay, cutie?"

Alex wasn't sure if it was the spinning lights, the pulsing jaunt of the guitars, the seemingly impenetrable crowd, or the clean, earthy smell of fresh sweat on the man that made him pay attention once more to Little Alex.

"I'm Paco, and you are?"

Alex took Paco's meaty hand in his fist and let him pump it several times, watching the veins flex under a tattoo of a supremely pissed off-looking rooster. Perhaps he didn't need another drink after all. "Alex. What's on your mind, Paco?"

Paco parted his thick lips to reveal a grinning set of perfect white teeth. "Just checking on you. I mean, you look like a smart guy. I'm sure you can take care of yourself."

Alex smiled. Paco had loosened his grip but not released him entirely. "You look like… a bad idea."

"That's not the worst thing I've been called." He laughed, squeezing Alex's hand one more time. When he began squeezing his pecs together, it was Alex's turn to laugh. "What? You like that? Touch, if you want."

Alex accepted the invitation, mapping the solid contours of the man's chest with his hand. He resisted brushing the guy's nipple. "It's too hot in here."

"Man, tell me about it. You want to go someplace?"

Alex shook his head. "Look, I'm not really… I mean thank you. You're very…" He squeezed Paco's bicep for good measure.

"That's me. Very. It pisses me off sometimes. Guys want the *very*, but they don't want to know the guy, you know?"

"I find that hard to believe," Alex slurred, unsure why.

"You think hot guys have it so easy?"

"You think you're hot?"

"I asked my question first."

They grinned at each other, which was the moment Alex knew he'd be accepting Paco's offer to walk him home. It wasn't until Paco pulled him close and started kissing him a block from his building that he knew this wasn't going to work. He was too tired. Too drunk, and no amount of liquor had eased his confusion over what the hell had transpired at Jago's. He politely declined Paco's offer to blow him in the next side street, exchanged one last sloppy kiss with the man, then continued on to his apartment alone. It wasn't until he fished his keys from his pocket that he noticed his wallet was gone.

CHAPTER THREE

Alex pulled himself through the doors of Café No Mismo the next morning just in time to catch Victoria's sharp look.

She rounded the counter and grabbed him by both arms. "I was worried! You don't seem to be in bad shape, but my God!"

"Victoria, I'm sorry, I can explain."

She offered him a blank stare before she continued. "No need. Your friend told me everything. These protests are getting out of hand—and I support them, but not when my staff get hurt. Are you sure you don't need another day off? I'll manage without you for a day or two."

"My… my friend?"

"Short, tanned fellow. I think his name was Jacob, or Jago or something? He came down to tell me in person. It was strange, but sweet. Is he, umm…?"

"No," Alex said quickly. True, this conversation must have taken place before Jago had cast him out with the fury of the Archangel Michael, but how had he known where to go or who to talk to? "We are just friends." If that, he qualified in his head.

"Okay, fine. Take today off, at least. I know I'm fussing—"

"I can't take time off. I got robbed last night."

"I'm sorry… What? How?"

Alex rolled his eyes. "The kind of boy who's a bad idea."

"I see. You *are* feeling better then. Look, go home. I'll pay you for today, just—"

"Victoria? I'm good, really. Reporting for duty." He raised his hand in a mock salute, deliberately keeping his wrist limp.

"Please," she answered. "The last thing we need in here is more uniforms. Have you eaten? If you're going to work, you're going to eat. Hold on."

Thanking her, Alex sat at one of the tables in the corner. Café No Mismo served the best pan con tomate within four blocks of Plaza Mayor, and when Victoria returned with a plate of it, he savoured each bite, chasing it with the long espresso she'd brought alongside.

Monday's quiet trickle of customers gave them a chance to start on the week's prep, while No Mismo's front window had one of the best views of the plaza. By one o'clock, he'd served barely a half-dozen customers. He skewered an olive and a spicy pepper to the last anchovy and set it on the platter while Victoria put the last touches on the new fixed price lunch.

"Beef cheek?" Alex asked.

"Try it. You'll die."

When she popped a tender morsel into his mouth, Alex nearly did, moaning with pleasure. What he wouldn't have given for a glass of Bobal to go with it.

"I told you. How are those gildas?"

"Slimy, and my hands smell like anchovy."

Victoria plucked one from the platter and inhaled the combination in one bite. She tilted her head from side to side. "Hmm, we'll get there."

"Didn't you come back from San Sebastián raving about these?" Alex asked, scrubbing his hands and signalling to a young lady customer he'd be with her shortly. They weren't San Sebastián yet, but at least the police weren't arresting them for propagating Basque cuisine. He sent the customer on her way with a cheerful smile, sandwich in hand.

"Well, hello again."

Alex looked up to see who Victoria was talking to, a knot forming in his stomach as he spied Jago, who stood red-faced, shooting him small, embarrassed glances, even as he tried to return Victoria's smile. "Hello. I'd like a vermouth, and do you have a blanco y negro?"

"Give me a few minutes." Victoria shot Alex a conspiratorial look as she absconded to the back table, baguette and two types of sausage in hand. "Alex?"

"Got it," he said, scooping ice into a glass and looking for the orange slices.

"How are you feeling?" Jago asked, his hands thrust deep into his pockets.

"Fine, thank you. Sweet or dry?"

"Dry. Alex?"

The two watched each other from beneath darkened brows, hesitant to speak as Alex poured.

"I only meant for you to get out of my room. Not the apartment."

Alex slid the drink across the bar. "You sounded a bit more forceful than that."

"You gave me a shock. I'm sorry, it's not an excuse for shouting at you like that. I…" Jago shot a nervous look toward Victoria as she piled the bread high with red and black meat. "I didn't know what you'd think."

"Think about what?"

"Some people think it's a creepy hobby."

Alex shook his head, none the wiser. "What is?"

"Taxidermy. Stuffing animals. Birds, mostly."

"*That's* what you were doing? That's your big secret?"

Jago smiled shyly, lifting the drink to his lips. "So now you know. And now you think I'm like Norman Bates in *Psycho*, right?"

"Not unless you're planning to don old woman drag and corner me with a knife in the shower."

"Gee, thanks for spoiling!" Victoria chirped, returning with a thick blanco y negro stuffed with sausage. "That'll be—"

"On the house." Alex turned quickly to Victoria. "It's the least I can do, for yesterday. I mean, before… you know what I mean."

"It's more than he can do," Victoria said with bone-dry intonation. "Someone got robbed last night."

"You *what?*" The way Jago's tone matched Victoria's was uncanny.

"It's not a big deal. My own stupid fault. I got drunk."

Victoria rolled her eyes. "Ooh, boy."

"Yes, remember your boss is standing right there." Jago smirked again.

"Okay, well not *that* drunk, maybe—"

"I think this would be an excellent time for someone's first break," said Victoria. "Don't you, Jago?"

Jago nodded with approval. "In that case, another vermouth please."

"Orange juice will do just fine," Alex said quickly. "Please."

"Please."

"*Please!*" Victoria pointed to a table at the far end of the café. "Orange juice it is. Now *please*, before I ban you both?"

With an apologetic smile, Alex carried Jago's mountainous sandwich to the table, where Jago took gentle but firm hold of his hand.

"I mean it, Alex. I'm sorry I lost my temper. You caught me by surprise, but that's no excuse for it. I'm sorry."

"Okay, stop." Alex tried to ignore how reassuring it felt to have Jago's hand on his. "You're more than forgiven. Who knows? If you didn't let me spend the day at your flat, I might have spent it in hospital, and we know how you feel about those."

Jago rubbed his thumb over the back of Alex's knuckles as he let go. "Thanks for saying that. We need to be careful these days. All these protests? So many different people working out what they want this country to be and claiming their little parts of it. Old men trying to hold on to their power. The church. The king. The military. The Basques. Catalonia… It takes more than the devil's death to turn Hell into Heaven."

An orange juice appeared on the table to Alex's right with a soft bump, before Victoria greeted another customer—a regular he recognised—with a cheery hello. He took a sip of juice, watching for any movement in Jago's eyes. "It's getting better though, isn't it? We can more or less do what we want, in Madrid at least. *We* can do what we want without the law bothering us."

"Ah yes, *we*. Men like us. And the law? The magical law, changed just last year? Poof! 1979, we're legal. 1954, we weren't. 1932, we were. 1928, we weren't. 1822…"

"Sorry, is this a reverse history lesson?"

"Point being, the law doesn't mean shit. Men will fuck whether the law says they can or not, and police will beat them for it whether the law says they should or not. You can be a good little Catholic boy who loves his mother and says his rosary while yearning for the loins of men. So, you come to Madrid. You fuck your brains out. Maybe you fall in love. What happens when the little Catholic boy goes back home? Does he hide? Does he change? Who are you when you go back to Andalusia?"

The words weren't exactly revelatory, but Alex could see himself in them.

"So where exactly *are* you from?" Jago asked, taking a bite of his sandwich. "Oh, my god. Excuse me, but that is heaven. Try some?"

"I just ate. And Los Angeles."

Jago paused another bite halfway to his mouth. "What the fuck are you doing here?"

Alex nodded, teasing a smile. "Not the cool one. The one just outside Cordoba that would blow away with the dust in a strong enough storm."

Jago laughed. "That's cute. You should use that line next time you're on the prowl. It'll get their attention."

"What makes you think I don't?"

Jago washed down another bite of sandwich with his vermouth. "And are you a good Catholic boy who came to Madrid to fuck his brains out and occasionally get robbed? For real, by the way?"

Alex winced. "It was just a few hundred pesetas. No big deal."

"I hope you at least got a blow job for it."

"I got nothing for it. Just…" He pulled the used napkin from his pocket. "Ugh. Let me get rid of this. I'll be right back."

"That was his?"

"I think so," Alex said, not remembering how he'd come into possession of it and deciding that was for the best.

"Can I have it?"

"Why? What are you going to do with it?"

"What are you going to do? Throw it in the trash?"

"What else would I do?"

"In that case, it's no use to you. Can I have it?"

Alex shook his head with an incredulous smile and handed it over.

"I know. I have strange hobbies. So did Dali."

"Dali has strange everything."

"True, though he had decent taste in men, once upon a time."

"Wait, Dali's not queer."

"I assure you he is. Gala too. Bisexual or whatever you want to call it. Their marriage is genuine, but our nation's great Surrealist is as at home on the fruit tree as you or I."

Alex swirled his orange juice, unsure what to believe and wishing he had some vodka.

"What?" Jago asked.

"Just you. I mean, the way you speak. It's colourful, is all."

"A bit more colour in the world can only be a good thing, wouldn't you say? We lost too much colour under Franco. Especially in the south."

"And where are *you* from, exactly?"

"A small town, like you, outside Grenada. Fuente Vaqueros."

Alex paused his drink halfway to his lips.

"You've heard of it?"

"Of course I've heard of it. Lorca's hometown."

"Ah, yes, Lorca, our great poet. You're directing *Blood Wedding*, aren't you? How could I forget?"

"I am, in my own way."

"Meaning what?"

"It's more of a dance piece. One woman, my friend Joanna. It's an interpretation."

Jago mumbled something through another bite of his sandwich, hurriedly swallowing it before clarifying. "Change it."

"What?"

"The movie Saura's making? Have you heard about this?"

"Yes…"

"It's about a dance company producing *Blood Wedding*. He's all but finished it."

Alex pressed his fingertips harder into the cool glass of his drink.

"You know? Carlos Saura, the filmmak—"

"I said I'd heard about it." He caught a look from Victoria and instantly lowered his voice. "I mean… that's great. It might make people more interested in our show."

"I'm sorry. I shouldn't have said that. I'm not trying to… When do you open?"

"Two weeks and a bit."

"Ah! You see? Ignore me. Saura's film won't be out until at least next year. If anyone's heard of it, like you said, it will probably just make them more curious."

"Honestly, I'm more worried about our timeline."

"Feeling the pinch, mister director?" Jago squeezed the sides of his glass, leaving fingerprints.

"I'm *feeling* frustrated. There's another production hogging the space and…" From the corner of his eye, Alex watched Vicente take off his sunglasses as he strode toward the counter carrying his football kit bag. "Over here!"

"Hey." Vicente pulled up a seat backwards at the table and straddled it. "Big night? I stopped by but you weren't home. Didn't answer the phone."

"I was out."

"Getting fucked?"

"Getting robbed."

"*What?*"

"I really wish people would stop saying that."

"Damn, I'm sorry, man. You know, never mind. I've got those lighting cue changes you asked for and… Sorry, hi." Vicente offered his hand to the bemused stranger at their table.

"Jago."

Alex watched them shake mismatched hands, Jago's tanned and smooth, Vicente's pale and shrouded with sandy hair. The combination was kind of sexy. "This is Vicente, our stage manager."

"You must be good. I know Alex is a perfectionist."

Vicente raised an eyebrow at Alex.

"He's also banging our star," Alex said.

"Banging? Fuck you." Vicente lightly punched Alex's arm. "It's been almost a year."

"I know." Alex laughed. "That was for that look. Don't think I didn't see it."

"And where, may I ask, is your star?" asked Jago.

"Resting at home. She wants to give it everything she's got tonight."

"Oh? You're rehearsing?"

"Like I said, two weeks." Alex watched Victoria approach them with a small platter of meats, cheeses, bread, and several of the gildas. He turned to Vicente. "Did you order?"

"He did not," answered Victoria. "This is now your lunch break. Twenty more minutes, mister director. Good to see you, handsome." She patted Vicente on the shoulder.

"Awww, thank you so much," he beamed, looking over the snacks. "You didn't have to do this."

Victoria left them with no further comment. Alex couldn't deny Vicente's way with women, and his naivety was one of his sweetest qualities. He'd never quite clued on to Victoria's attempts to lure him back into Alex's love life. When they'd broken up, Alex had heard nothing else from her for almost a month.

Jago picked up one of the gildas. "I haven't had one of these in… must be ten years."

Alex watching him pop the entire pepper, anchovy, olive monstrosity in his mouth in one bite, then slide the skewer from his lips. He couldn't. No way. The briny smell of the fish still burned his nostrils. "Ten years? Wait, how old are you?"

"How old do you think?"

Vicente shrugged. "Twenty…. wait."

Jago began tilting his hand toward the ceiling, gesturing for them to guess higher.

"Thirty-two?"

"Thirty-eight."

"What?" Alex snapped. "No way."

"Christ, man, what's your secret?" Vicente asked.

Jago smiled with a broad spread of flawless white teeth. "Curiosity and an appreciation of beauty."

Alex shook his head. This guy…

"Also, water, sleep, and very few sweets. No Christ, though."

"More like magick," Vicente said with a laugh.

"Magick can't fix everything, my friend." Jago drained the last of his vermouth, putting the glass down firmly on the table.

Alex ate a slice of Manchego, unsure how to answer that. "Lighting cues, you said?"

"Yeah." Vicente fished a notebook from his kit bag and set an open page in front of Alex. "We can try them tonight. Shouldn't take long to set up."

"May I come watch?"

The two of them looked up at Jago, making no effort to hide their surprise.

"If that's all right. I have a special fondness for *Blood Wedding*. I would love to see what you're doing with it."

If only for a second, Alex found himself confused by the look that crossed Vicente's face. It was defensive, as if their unfinished work had been cornered for some premature critical scrutiny.

"We're still working things out," he said quietly. "I'd be embarrassed to—"

"Embarrassed? You should never be embarrassed just because the work isn't finished. You told me yourself, you're worried about having so little time to prepare. I'm not asking to judge. Only watch and help if I can."

"We don't need help," Vicente said, eating a slice of sausage.

In truth, Alex wasn't so sure. Curiosity and an appreciation of beauty?

"Sure," he said at last. "Seven o'clock, Cervantes Culture Forum, studio—"

"Seriously?" Vicente burned him with a glare before turning back to Jago. "I mean, no offense, man, but we've just met you and—"

Jago lifted another gilda from the plate, turning the skewer in his fingers as if studying the strange ingredients impaled on it. "*Everything that can cut a man's body. A beautiful man, tasting the fullness of life*... I've always thought that line danced on its own. I'd love to see how it dances on your stage, if only that. You say you owe me? This would more than pay your debt."

"I... okay, sure? I guess?"

"Uh, excuse me," Vicente said, raising a hand as Jago swallowed the gilda in one smooth bite. "I'm also still here. Do I not get a vote in this?"

Jago smiled. "You're right. I'm sorry. It was rude to put you on the spot. Another time, perhaps?"

Alex winced as his mind leapt to the notes he'd made after their last rehearsal. "No, tonight would be great." He turned to Vicente, hoping his apology looked as sincere as his desperation. "It couldn't hurt."

Vicente curled his fingers so hard, Alex was sure he'd scratch the table. "Okay," he said at last, getting up. "You're the boss. I'll see you both at seven."

Alex nodded, trying to regain some semblance of directorial authority. He was close to calling out 'love you,' a habit he'd tried to break himself of since Joanna had entered their lives, but he managed to bite his tongue.

"Your friend doesn't like me."

"He's protective. Don't worry, he'll come around."

"I don't want to cause you trouble. You need him more than you need me."

"It's settled." Alex popped another piece of Manchego into his mouth, glad he'd talked Victoria out of her plan to find a new supplier. "He's just worried if these new cues look like shit, he'll look a fool."

"All art looks foolish until it's done."

"That's what I try to tell him." Alex sighed. "He's not such a creative guy, but he's a genius with tech."

"That's perfect. Too many mediocre creative talents out there. Not enough true genius."

"Thanks?"

"Not you. At least, I trust you're not mediocre. I can usually read these things."

Alex caught an evil eye from Victoria. "I've got to get back."

"Until tonight then?" Jago took Alex's hand in his and with a sweeping bow, kissed the back of it.

Alex's eyes widened. "Until tonight."

Jago grinned, tipping his head to Victoria as he departed.

Alex watched him cross the Plaza Mayor until he disappeared under the portico leading to Sol. He'd forgotten to give him their room number for the rehearsal, but Jago seemed the type who could figure these things out without too much trouble.

"Someone's cup overfloweth," Victoria teased.

Alex cleared their table, picking up Jago's glass and remembering the request for the used napkin.

CHAPTER FOUR

"It's only been twenty minutes," Joanna pointed out. "Maybe his train's delayed?"

"Vicente's never late." Alex tapped his pen on the edge of his notepad, wishing it could crack open something in his skull. "He's not with you?"

"Football," they said together as Alex remembered.

A loud knock came from the house doors behind him.

"Hello?" called Jago, whose instincts had served him well. "Is this the Women's Temperance Society meeting or is that a few doors down?"

"You came." Alex got to his feet, giving their guest a warm hug. "Joanna, you didn't meet Jago?"

"I don't think so," she said, extending a hand. "A pleasure."

"All mine, I promise you. I've heard you're the true talent driving this venture."

"Have you? I've not heard anything about you at all. Though we saw you at the film the other night. *Pepi, Luci, Bom?*"

"Vicente didn't say anything?" asked Alex. "They met this afternoon."

"Briefly," added Jago. "I don't think I made the best impression."

"I haven't seen him since this morning," Joanna said. "Perhaps they went for beers after the match?"

"That's no reason to be late." Alex nodded at Jago. "Not in Vicente's book, anyway."

"Well, I'm sorry *I'm* late," said Jago. "I had to finish something at home that couldn't wait."

"Jago's into taxid..." Alex bit his lip. "I'm sorry, I shouldn't have said that."

"Taxidermy, yes." Jago smiled at Joanna. "I don't usually advertise the fact, but I have a feeling you're my kind of people, if that's not too bold of me."

"You do have that sexy, young Anthony Perkins thing happening," she teased. "But taxidermy? How interesting."

"Please, don't let me interrupt. I'm here to watch."

"There's not much to watch until Vicente arrives. Damn it!"

"Sweetheart," cautioned Joanna. "He'll be here. Did he give you the cues?"

"He did," Jago reminded him. "Perhaps if you give them to me, I could help? I'm no Vicente, but I can at least make sure we see you."

Joanna laughed while Alex shook his head. It beat the hell out of waiting.

"From the top then?" he asked. "I was hoping for a full run tonight."

"I'm ready if you boys are."

Jago nodded. "Just tell me where to go."

Alex directed him to the tech booth, resettling in his seat as Joanna took her mark. Here went bloody nothing, then.

*   *   *

"What do you mean, it's not embarrassing?" asked Alex, quoting Jago's rave of the century.

"I mean, it's a functional, sometimes beautiful telling of a story I know very well. It might be a little unclear to someone who doesn't, but there is only so much you can do without dialogue in the space of an hour."

"There's only so much *I* can do in an hour, you mean," Joanna pouted with a touch of ire.

"Exactly," said Alex. "And she's on stage the whole time without a break."

"Your star isn't the problem." Jago shot a glance at Joanna that Alex supposed was a peace offering. "There are no problems as such. It's just… safe?"

"Safe?"

"Great," Joanna said. "So, I'm supposed to dress like a nun and slay it out on the bongos?"

Jago covered his face with his hands. "I shouldn't have said anything. I'm sorry."

"Well, you did, and if you said it, at least some of the audience will think it. We haven't put all this work in just to be safe." Alex turned to Joanna. "Right?"

She shrugged, sipping more of her water. "Let's have it, then."

Jago offered them a tiny bow of contrition before continuing. "I just mean you're telling a story about a cycle of violence and revenge."

"Would you prefer a nun with a sword or a rifle?"

"Joanna…"

"The props don't matter, though the nun's habit is up to you. The way I see it, you can take it in one of two directions. Either you take on the energy and representation of both families in the story, manifesting a kind of self-destruction in the search for love—most likely of one's self, since you're a one-woman show—or, you go the meta route."

Alex winced. How he hated that word, meta.

"A beautiful dance, rising from the broken, bloodied grounds of this feud. The battle isn't one between warring families. But between beauty and ruin, as one feeds the other."

Alex studied Jago's face, as if some line or twitch in his expression might reveal him taking the piss out of them, or reaching for platitudes that would numb Joanna's dance into mediocrity. But it *was* mediocre. That was Jago's point, and both Joanna and Alex knew it.

"We could try that," Joanna said quietly.

"I'm not sure it's what Lorca had in mind."

"Are you sure?" Jago asked. "You might be surprised."

Hell, they had the space for another ninety minutes. It couldn't hurt to try something new. "All right," Alex said. "From the top."

"And change what?" Joanna asked. "You don't want me to make it up as I go from scratch, surely?"

"Of course not," said Jago. "The choreography you have is… fine. You just need to emphasise what's underneath it. Let that rise through your movements. I mean, from the booth, I can see you, but… if I may?"

Alex caught on. "You want to sit out here while I work the lights?"

Jago shook his head, waving the suggestion away. "Forget the lights. Forget the music, even. Right now, I just… I'm sorry, I'm directing over you. I'll stop."

"I'd like you to finish your thought." Alex knew he should have been pissed off, but he could also admit when he was intrigued.

"Take the scene where the Bride accepts the Bridegroom's gift, the wax wreath of orange blossoms. She despises it and all it represents, yes? His wealth, security, safety... In her eyes, it's not a decoration, but a cage, closed on her against her will."

Joanna shook her head. "I know all this."

"Of course, but are you feeling it? I see your rage in the moment. I see your rejection of the gift, but not of the bondage it represents. Of order, the favoured virtue of the Fascists."

Alex ignored the faint rumble in his stomach. He was too fixed on the dark, animated face of this near-stranger who now spoke of their play—his favourite part of their play—as if it were his own. Damn it, he was right. "Just the orange blossoms, then." He gave Joanna the nod.

Without a word, Joanna braced herself, lifted her arms high and began moving to the silent, memorised score. When she lifted the imagined wreath from her head, she threw it to the ground with such force that even the silent movement startled Alex. Feeling Jago squeeze his hand, he turned. Jago was grinning all over, completely in his element.

"Dark clouds," he said, referencing the script. "A cold wind inside you. Doesn't everyone feel it? *Make* them feel it."

They continued like this until the scene was done. Jago's notes grew scarcer and scarcer as Joanna found them on her own, until she at last lay on the floor, hands resting on her throat. Jago's hand remained in Alex's until they both applauded earnestly.

"That was..." None of the words Alex fished for seemed adequate. "That was great, Joanna. Really, it was great."

"Yes, what was that?" Vicente stood at the top of the steps, leaning against the house doors, his arms folded.

"What happened to you?" Alex asked.

"Train strike. Had to get a lift with Miguel and then *he* had a breakdown on the highway outside Fuenlabrada. Can you believe it? Joanna?"

She got to her feet, slow and steady as if they were new to her.

"How are you feeling?" Jago asked.

"Good! Good, I…" Joanna reached for her water and sipped. "I felt… You really liked it?"

"I said I did," Alex answered.

"So did I," added Vicente. "I just want to know what it was."

"Jago was helping us with the rehearsal. You weren't here, and he has some experience—"

"I did nothing." Jago raised his hands in protest. "It's your choreography. Your performance. I just reminded you of what was already there. But I should let you get to work."

"You won't stay and try one more scene?" Joanna asked, not taking her eyes off Jago.

"You don't need me, and I'd hate to be in the way. You've a fine talent in good hands, mister director."

Alex accepted a firm hug and a kiss on the cheek before Jago bounded up the stairs.

"Nice to see you again, Vicente."

Vicente forced a smile as the doors closed behind their guest. "So, we're in collaboration now?"

"Nothing of the sort," Alex said, dismissing the idea with a wave of his hand. "It's one of Jago's favourite plays. He asked to watch a rehearsal and I owed him."

"I know. I was there. And what do you mean, you owed him?"

"I got caught up in a protest just as the police arrived. It was bad. Jago pulled me out and took care of me."

Vicente's face was quizzical as he approached. "You didn't tell me about that. Did he tell you about that? Joanna? Joanna?"

Joanna was already sweeping across the stage with elegant, powerful moves that accentuated her long limbs, as if snatching up scraps for the story unfolding in her imagination and consuming them whole, each one another morsel that made up the dance. Alex could still see traces of his choreography, but only just. That suited him. It was Joanna who brought a dancer's mind to their stage. Right now, she was reinventing their work, making her flow look effortless, a woman possessed by poetry.

"Joanna?"

"Shhh." Alex didn't even notice the glare Vicente gave him. He was too transfixed, absorbed by each graceful movement. He hadn't dared presume they'd achieve anything so grand as expressing Lorca's poetry through dance, but this was so close.

Joanna quickened her steps, arms sweeping through the air, legs arcing gracefully over the few props they'd put on stage, her gaze fixated—on what, Alex couldn't say. Something that didn't exist in that room. Possibly not in their world.

Joanna let out a strong, fast exhale and dragged her outstretched hand across her body, beneath the collarbone, grasping at her shoulders before repeating the action. Into this rhythm she brought the same clawing movement, this time along her inner thigh, tearing into what would be the wedding dress, once she was in costume. But Alex saw no rage in her face. There was joy, even freedom, but none of the anger that had been present during her dance with the orange blossoms. Had she wandered off script?

"Alex? *Joanna!*" Vicente raced to the stage, gently taking Joanna and pulling her away from the spot where blood had trickled onto the floor.

The shouts snapped Alex from his dream state, while Joanna shook her head, looking down at her scratched thighs and the ruined legs of her body stocking.

"My god, Jo, are you okay?"

"She's not okay, she's bleeding. Call a doctor."

"No, I…" Joanna held her bloodstained fingers up to her face, as if surprised to find them there. "How? I don't feel anything."

"Seriously?" Vicente pointed to the long scratch down her thigh. "You don't feel this?"

"Stop fussing and give me a minute, will you?" Joanna nimbly got to her feet and with no show of pain, disappeared backstage.

"What the hell?" Vicente fairly hissed. "Okay, *he* is not to come to another one of these, is that—"

"Woah, hold on. I assume you mean Jago? Because *he* didn't go anywhere near her."

"There's blood on the damn stage, Alex. Jo's blood."

"And Jo's not…" Alex paused, trying to be tactful.

"No, I'm not." Joanna's voice was cold, detached, and matter-of-fact as she emerged from behind the flat, now dressed in a simple t-shirt and short shorts. "I just scratched myself. It wasn't deep. See? Already gone."

They stared at the smooth, pale skin on the inside of her thigh. It wasn't bleeding nor broken, nor even bruised.

"How?" Vicente asked. "You scratched yourself. You said that."

"Perhaps I didn't break skin? I mean, I didn't feel anything."

"There's blood on the stage, Joanna," Alex reminded her.

"Clearly, not mine."

"That's not particularly any better."

Joanna shook her head, the first signs of exasperation showing on her face. "I don't know what to tell you. Let's just mop the stage and forget about it, all right? Perhaps a drink somewhere?"

"A drink?"

"I'm rather tired."

Alex looked at Vicente, who shrugged.

Joanna's eyes were animated with excitement as she spoke. "Just let me work on this in private. I'll have something amazing to show you tomorrow night, I promise."

"How can you promise—"

"Alex, I don't know how, I just know I can. I'm feeling… Tomorrow, yes?"

Alex and Vicente exchanged looks again, knowing they'd be foolish to try to dissuade her.

"I'll get a mop," Vicente said, retreating backstage.

Joanna at last stepped down, graceful and elegant as she'd been throughout the dance. She took Alex by both hands and kissed his cheek. "You're cleverer than you know."

"You think so?"

"I've always known it." She raised her eyebrows mischievously. "Now, I'm certain."

"Thanks, I think?"

Together, the three of them removed any trace of the bizarre event, picked up their bags and crossed the darkened courtyard of the Culture Forum to the streets that lead into Chueca. They tossed around a few suggestions for dinner, most of them more expensive than they could afford before settling on Angel Sierra on Chueca Square. Joanna ordered them each an enormous gin and tonic along with some croquettes which wouldn't nearly line their stomachs enough. Gin and tonics were the last thing Alex wanted to drink, but he humoured her, adding some patatas bravas to even things out. What he really wanted was flamenquín. A huge, greasy piece of pork, wrapped in ham and deep fried would fortify him through a half-dozen gin and tonics.

Neither of the boys spoke, until Joanna, after ten minutes fawning over the café's history—"did you know it opened all the way back during the first war, and survived Franco and…"—said "Jago seems quite brilliant."

Alex felt his throat tighten, immediately wondering how to extricate himself from this topic. The silence it created grew thick with tension as a plate of croquettes and some potatoes slathered in spicy sauce landed on their table. The waiter had the good sense to hurry away.

Joanna raised her eyebrows. "Gosh. Never mind."

"No," Alex said. "No, you might be right. He certainly seems to know *Blood Wedding* well enough."

"Everyone knows *Blood Wedding*." Vicente put a croquette and several pieces of sauce-slathered potato on his plate. "I'm glad he helped."

Alex winced. Yep, his grandmother's flamenquín sounded pretty good around now, if only because it would shut them up with a mash of pork, crumbs, ham and good commonsense discretion. "Yeah, I think he did. Nice guy."

"Nice guy," Vicente echoed, half-heartedly.

Joanna took another sip of her drink. "You said he pulled you out of the Basque protest on the weekend? That was brave."

"Brave?"

"I just mean, he's not a big guy. Wiry, though."

"How do you reason that?" Vicente asked, taking a drink.

"Forearms, my love. He had his sleeves rolled up at the rehearsal. Those veins?" She wiggled her eyebrows at Alex.

"Are you suggesting something?"

"I'm suggesting you do what makes you happy," she replied. "Nothing more."

"Are you sure he's not making *you* happy?"

"I really don't think I'm his type, do you?"

"Right," Vicente said, getting up. "I need to piss."

"Go find yourself a nice bored masochistic housewife," Joanna said, playfully.

Vicente tossed her a half-hearted smile and retreated to the small door leading to the toilets.

"Holy shit," whispered Alex.

"Relax. Vicente will come around, *if* there's anything to come around to. I mean, you've only just met this boy, correct?"

"Yes, and don't say it like we're dating. I don't know what you'd call it. We're not even friends. He's…"

"Your muse?"

"Don't be pretentious."

"What? You don't think he looks like Lorca? Just a bit? Same nose. Same bright eyes. Same small stature."

"Are you joking? You said he looked like Anthony Perkins barely an hour ago. Besides, Lorca, may he rest in peace, had to be at least twenty pounds heavier *and* ten years older when he died."

"So? Jago's a younger, prettier model, with muscles. I'm not seeing a downside."

"He's from a farming region."

"I rest my case."

"Lorca's hometown, actually."

Joanna smiled quizzically. "That's an interesting—"

"—coincidence? Yes, it is. Joanna, that's *all* it is."

"He could be a relative. A distant one, at least. Maybe that's why he was so invested in our little show."

"I doubt it. Why wouldn't he say so?"

"Probably just too modest. Look, we're getting ahead of ourselves. Do you like him? I assume yes, since you brought him to rehearsal."

"Of course I like him." Alex popped a croquette into his mouth, praying to any saint who would listen that Joanna would do the same. Or at least drink more. Or complain of a headache and go home. "He looked after me that day, I told you."

"You didn't tell us much, but go on."

"Then he... I don't know. It was strange. Scary, in a way."

The motor powering Joanna's interrogation seemed to pause. "In what way?"

"I went looking for him in his apartment. I found him in this small office, full of... I don't know how to describe it, except that it creeped me out. Old books, stuffed birds, tapestries with these strange symbols on the wall, a human skull, even—God knows if it was real—and the smell? Like Moroccan incense mixed with straw."

"Sounds positively fascinating."

"I suppose it was, until he saw me and screamed at me. I mean, he *screamed* at me to get out."

"After he spent the day looking after you?" Joanna shook her head, taking another sip of her drink. "Sorry, I'm lost."

"Me too. I just left. Whatever his deal was, I couldn't stay."

"I get that."

"Then today he came by the café." Alex shrugged, spooning himself more potatoes. "He apologised. Said he was worried his taxidermy hobby would freak me out or something."

"So, he cared about what you thought, presumably because he wanted to see you again?" Joanna sipped again. "Sounds like an utter psychopath."

"You're glossing over the yelling."

"Yelling or screaming? There's a subtle difference."

Alex managed to hold back a growl. "Joanna…"

"Fine. He yelled, or screamed, or barked at you to get out of his apartment. Then what?"

"I left, of course. Although today he said he wasn't *actually* telling me to leave the apartment. Just that room."

"To which you had looked in uninvited, taking him by surprise."

"You're determined to not take my side in this, aren't you?"

"What side are we talking about? I don't know him, and this may sound esoterically bonkers to you, but all I'm hearing is that you caught a sensitive man who cares what you think of him doing something he wasn't ready to show you, and it seems to me like he's already forgiven you. Stop stressing. It's not like you walked in on him masturbating."

Alex swallowed, biting both lips. "I really wish Vicente hadn't told you about that."

Joanna laughed. "I'm sorry. It might not be a fairytale romance, but it's cute."

"Cute? That I walked in on… ugh!"

She smiled, taking hold of his wrist. "That you then dated for more than a year after, silly."

"What did I miss?"

Joanna and Alex gripped their drinks tighter, trying not to giggle as Vicente sat down. It gave them away immediately.

"Really?" Vicente asked, plating himself another croquette and some potatoes. "You're never gonna let that story go, are you?"

"Sorry, it tickles me." Joanna gave an innocent shrug, scooping up some of the bravas sauce on her fork, slipping it between her lips and moaning with soft appreciation.

"It's much better with the potatoes," Alex pointed out.

"I'm cutting my starches. Besides, I want to play with our choreography a bit more tonight. We're on the edge of something amazing here. I can feel it, can't you?"

Alex wasn't about to point out that he'd seldom seen her eat much of anything, but he still noticed the way she'd deflected his inquiry with her own question. "I did. I mean, I do."

Vicente's eyes moved from one of them to the other. "Don't get me wrong, you looked amazing, amor..."

She gave him a gracious smile.

"It's just, that guy—"

"Jago is his name," Alex interrupted. "He's not joining us at any more rehearsals. He asked to sit in on one and he did. What we do with it from here is up to us."

"Yes?" asked Joanna. "And what do you plan to do with him?"

"What do you mean?"

"Darling," She gripped Alex's shoulder, playfully jostling him back and forth. "He's gorgeous, and for whatever reason, interested in you. Then, there's the play. Didn't you feel something while he was watching?"

"Feel something?" Vicente's question was soaked with scepticism.

Joanna nodded. "It was like... I had every character inside my head all at the same time. I knew them all intimately. It should have felt confusing, but it didn't. It was just the opposite, like every thought and action had its own place and order, and it all just flowed into each movement."

"You're forgetting the blood. That's not a problem?"

"Forget about the blood, will you? I'm fine. I just know how I felt in that moment on stage. We all saw the difference it made.

Are we really going to just toss that away? I just want to….” Joanna let out a determined grunt when the words wouldn’t come.

“Are you okay?”

“Yes! Sorry. I just have a lot of energy right now. I’ve never felt like this. Like I’m drawing in and pushing out so much all at the same time. But it’s like… there’s something I need as well, and I’m not sure what that is.” She reached across the table and took Vicente’s wrist. “I need to find out. Will you at least understand that?”

Vicente shook his head, taking a long, slow sip of his drink. “If this is what you want, I won’t fight you.”

“Thank you, my love.”

“Okay. What does that mean, then? Do you want me to invite Jago to the next rehearsal? Or to the one after that?” Alex made no effort to hide the hesitation in his words, remembering only as he took the last croquette that he had no way of actually contacting Jago, short of trying to find his apartment again.

Joanna waved away his suggestion. “Let me play with it first. I need….” She covered her mouth, releasing her energy again in one great, muffled roar that was followed by a broad grin. “I’m excited! Aren’t you? I want to get started right away.”

Vicente signalled the waiter to bring their bill. “All right. I was just going to walk Alex home.”

“Me?”

“Do that,” Joanna said, snatching the bill from the table before either of them could grab it. “I’m going straight home. I need this.”

"Vicente," Alex protested. "I'm fine. No late-night stops at Black and White, I promise."

"Why don't you both go to Black and White?" Joanna suggested, passing the bill back to the waiter with some cash. "That way you can keep an eye on each other, and Vicente can beat the living hell out of the man who robbed you if you see him again."

"Are you saying I couldn't do that myself?"

"Or that I would?" Vicente winced at the suggestion.

"You two are no fun tonight." She raised her glass, its contents now mostly melted ice water and a sad slice of orange. "To our *Blood Wedding*."

The boys met her toast, drained their glasses in unison, and left the café. Joanna wrapped them each in an enormous hug, then shot off faster than either of them could have kept up.

"Will she be okay?"

"Oh yeah. Besides, she's made her mind up. The fight is hopeless." Vicente stepped out of the way of two drag queens whose wigs had been lacquered and stretched more than a foot in every direction. "Black and White won't open for another hour or two."

"I really don't feel like it, do you?"

"Come on then."

"What?"

"I promised you a walk home."

Alex smiled, suddenly happier for the invitation. They took their time, weaving through the streets of Chueca and watching the bands of two, three or more homos and other misfits darting from door to door in search of their night out. A surly Moroccan-looking bouncer admitted a pair of muscular, leather-clad kinksters to a darkened doorway while neon-coloured t-shirts with cut-off waists made a gaggle of freshly minted twinks impossible to miss. In Cordoba, or even Seville, they probably would have been detained, sent home, or worse. No matter how familiar it began to seem, watching Madrid's most colourful characters—straight, gay or otherwise—just going about their lives like the party would never end, always made Alex smile.

"I really hope you know what you're doing," Vicente said as they turned into his street. The words hadn't been accusatory or even cynical. Just concerned.

"I've been telling myself that since we started this. It'll be great. Trust me."

"I mean this guy."

"Come on, Vis. Really?"

"Don't 'come on, Vis' me. I do trust you." Vicente shook his head, turning toward a mixed group who'd burst into song at the end of the street. "Okay, I'll drop it. You're a big boy, and if you think he can help the play…"

Alex put a hand on Vicente's shoulder. "Thank you."

As they neared Alex's block, flashing red lights reflected off the walls overlooking a small side street—the same one where Alex had been robbed the night before. Behind an ambulance and two police bikes, they saw a small white car, crumpled at the front where it had hit the wall at obvious speed. Between the pulsing lights, Alex made out the thick shape of a man pinned against the wall by what remained of the hood.

"Jesus," Vicente said. "Hey, what are you doing?"

Alex felt Vicente tugging him back as he tried to get closer. "I just want to see."

"You're macabre, you know that?"

Macabre? It wasn't every day he saw fatal car accidents in the back streets of Chueca. He could just now make out the face. The bright colours of a rooster tattooed on the forearm… "Holy shit."

"You there, get back," one of the officers barked at them.

Alex tried to catch his breath as he allowed Vicente to drag him away.

"Man, why did you do that? What is wrong with you right now?"

"Vis, that was him."

"What? Who?"

"Paco… I mean, he said his name was… That was the guy who robbed me."

Vicente stared at him, lost for words. "I don't understand. The dead guy?"

"Yes, the dead guy, look."

"Look? How would I recognise—"

"Right. Forget it. I just—"

"You're sure?"

"*Yes.*"

"That's… Let's just go home."

Nothing else was said until they reached the front door of Alex's building, where Jago sat on the step, waiting with a full bottle of red wine.

"Hi," Alex said quietly. Vicente said nothing.

"Hey." Jago's smile quickly darkened. "Are you guys okay? You look like you've seen—"

"There was an accident," said Vicente. "It looked nasty."

"An accident?"

"Yeah, it's… it was bad." Questions turned in Alex's head like a wheel until he at last grabbed the most obvious one. "How did you find my house?"

"I'm sorry. Of course, this looks so rude of me. When I took you back to my place, I checked your wallet for your identity card. I swear, it was just in case I had to call a doctor."

"Ah. Okay, I guess."

"I'm sorry. I thought it would be a nice surprise."

"It's a surprise," Vicente said. "If you don't mind, man, we're kind of shaken up. Maybe another time?"

"Of course, of course. Here." Jago handed Vicente the bottle of wine. "A peace offering? I'll leave you be."

"Wait," said Alex, quickly. "It's okay."

"Seriously?" Vicente asked, his mask of civility slipping for just a second.

"Vis, I'm fine. You go up. I'll be there in a bit." Alex handed him the keys. Vicente paused, giving Jago one last sceptical look before making good on his promise to trust that Alex knew what he was doing.

"He really doesn't like me, does he?"

"He doesn't know you," insisted Alex. "Honestly, neither do I."

"Perhaps we should do something about that."

The two of them watched an ambulance drive by the end of the street, presumably carrying the body of the deceased Paco. Alex didn't see any reason to share the victim's identity with Jago. The air seemed fresher, somehow, for its departure.

Alex felt a shiver go through him. "I think Vicente would have kittens if I invited you up."

"You know, I didn't really bring the wine for him. Perhaps he can spare you for ten minutes? Perhaps fifteen?"

"Twenty?" Alex teased.

"You're the one with somewhere to be. Or someone to be with."

"Vicente? No, that ended a while ago."

"But he's still loyal to you." Jago took Alex by the hand. "I promise not to keep you out too late."

They weaved swiftly through the crowds on either side of the Gran Via before Jago led Alex into the now quiet streets of the theatre district, pulling him along like a child excited to share some hidden secret. As they reached Plaza Santa Ana, Jago at last turned to face him, his face a stupid, lopsided grin.

"Look!" Jago pointed at the posters on the edifice of the Teatro Espanol.

"*Blood Wedding*?" Alex read. "Yes, I know. It just closed."

"And it will open again, with your show."

"Okay, first of all, not here, and secondly, our show's a dance show, not a straight play."

"Like Saura's film? Dance, yes, but it's the same story."

Alex tensed his fists. "What is your point?"

"I just want you to tell me why. Why this story? Why this same play that everyone is doing?"

"Because it's one of the great—"

"Stop! I beg you to stop, please. Yes, 'one of the great landmarks of the Spanish theatre blah, blah, blah. What about the great works of Goya or Velazquez? Where are they?"

Alex shrugged. "In museums?"

"Exactly. Slowly rotting and dying in museums while the nation whose spirit they supposedly capture pays to spend a few minutes gawking at them. Tourists too, just to say they've seen them, which is worse. Imagine, going around the world, looking for pieces of art, just to say, 'oh yes, darling, *we* saw that one in Paris last year. '*Tick!*' It's nauseating, not that having them in the private collections of the obscenely rich would be any better."

"I…" Alex hesitated as a couple passed them. He watched Jago take out a cigarette and light it before offering him one. He declined. "I never thought of it like that."

"Of course not. We're not supposed to ask those questions or say those things. Not supposed to disrespect our great artistic saints. Yet we disrespect them constantly. We put them away to gather dust and die, pretending they still have life because we look at them every now and again in museums, or theatres."

"I don't think that's true."

"No?"

"Okay, so a young painter goes to the Prado, spends a few hours looking at Goyas and Velasquez…" The plural eluded him. "It lives because we keep it alive in new work."

"Ah! New work, yes. Then tell me, Alex. You have a brilliant mind, a brilliant dancer, and a brilliant friend to support you. Why aren't you making new work?"

"We are. Our *Blood Wedding*'s about—"

Jago pointed to the theatre again. "Look at this place. Inside, it's one of the most beautiful buildings in Madrid. Have you been?"

"No."

"Right. Because it's maddeningly expensive. A glorified museum where rich people pay to see the same stories done the same way, over and over and over again, pretending they're patrons of our great national arts. It's beyond fucking bourgeois, and it's not culture."

"I thought you liked *Blood Wedding*?"

"It is Lorca at the apex of his powers, which is why I despise what it's become. But why are you doing it?"

Alex shook his head, a pitch in that moment far from top of mind. "Because of Lorca? A tribute, I guess? We're both from Andalusia…"

"So? I'm from his home town. Try harder."

"He captures something. The stupid prejudices and violence of rural minds. Provincial minds."

"You've read a lot of his poems, I suppose? His other plays?"

"Of course."

"Then why would you think he despises Andalusia as you do?"

The accusation, if Alex could call it that, stung hard. Yet there was no cruelty or cynicism in Jago's face. He'd been sincere, even sympathetic.

"I don't despise it."

"No? Lorca celebrated the romance and beauty of his homeland, but you?" Jago shook his head grimly. "Why do you so despise it?"

Alex felt cornered. He didn't know why he was justifying himself in the first place, and yet the question, now it was out, bothered the hell out of him. "Because it despised me first."

"And there's another old story. So, you run away to Madrid? Another young, outcast maricón in a city awash with them?" Jago mimed a yawn.

"What do you want me to say? It's like you said. *Blood Wedding* is Lorca at the apex of his powers. I want to see if we can make it dance. Is that so strange? Or maybe I'm just doing a story people know so they come see it—come see *us*. And what do you care? Are you a director or a choreographer or something?"

"No."

"Exactly. You know what? I'm going home. Thank you again for everything. For the wine. It was great meeting you and having you at rehearsal, but we're fi—"

"None of them see you though, do they?"

"What's that supposed to mean?"

"The people you're trying to be. The people you would be if you only trusted yourself, but of course you don't. So you cling to an old story from the very place you despise, the very place they ridicule you for, if not to your face—"

"Oh, come on, enough!"

"—and you hope they'll notice you for it? Respect you for it?" Jago shook his head, his sympathy at last seeming more than a little patronising as he drew close enough for Alex to feel the heat from his body. "Your Joanna understands the play's emotions. Its rage and violence. Do you understand yours?"

Alex wasn't sure why he allowed Jago so close to him their noses were touching. Or why he hadn't taken his eyes off Jago's stare since his last outburst. "One more time. Why do you care?"

"Because those who have the ability deserve every chance to be great. To share that ability with others. So, as good as it is, as much as I love it, if this old story isn't lighting that fire in you?" Jago's lips brushed his before he withdrew with a deep bow. "You have my blessing to change it."

"Your blessing?" Alex laughed.

"Do I flatter myself?"

"Maybe. Hell, Joanna thinks you look like Lorca, but…"

"A little sexier, I hope?" Jago grinned, admiring the theatre's façade one more time before turning back and giving a mocking flex of his biceps that made Alex laugh.

"I'm sure he would approve. He'd probably sleep with you."

"Hah! All the great poets are peerless narcissists at heart. They never found his body, did they? Perhaps that's the story you really wish to tell, and I will be your Lorca."

Alex laughed, shaking his head. "I don't think he was as fit as you."

"Artistic license?" Jago's smile turned shy. "And thank you. I am just as I appear."

Alex felt a tinge of guilt for wondering just how Jago appeared under his shirt. "I should get home."

Jago stepped closer. "May I see you again?"

It didn't take Alex long to find an answer. "Rehearsal? You made quite an impression on Joanna."

"To be honest, she made one on me. So, yes, rehearsal, but… in other places too?" Jago's smile widened, even as he looked down at his feet. Before Alex could pretend to stop him, their lips had brushed once more, and Alex took him in a deep, open kiss. At last, it felt as if Jago were relaxing in his arms.

"I think I'd like that," Alex finished the thought.

Jago's grin lit up his face as he squeezed Alex's hand and withdrew into the night. "At rehearsal then? Same time and place tomorrow?"

"Yes," Alex called. "The same."

Jago was already across the square, and if Alex wanted Vicente to not tear his flesh off one strip at a time, he'd need to be just as swift. He was home and ringing his front door bell within ten minutes. When no answer came, he tried again, then knocked on the door. Still no answer. Another knock, louder this time, before he tried the bell again.

"All right, all right! Good heavens, who is it?" Lucia announced herself before throwing open the door and fixing him with such a glare, Alex was certain he'd just been cursed. "A fine time of night this is to be waking me up! You haven't lost your keys, I hope?"

"No. I'm sorry, I gave them to my friend. I buzzed. I thought he'd let me up."

The old woman shook her head and stepped aside, closing the door behind him. "A friend?"

"Yes, Lucia, a friend. Someone I know very well."

She nodded begrudging acceptance. "Goodnight then." She shuffled back to her apartment, closing her door with a loud *CLUNK*. What the hell was wrong with Vicente?

He bounded up the stairs two at a time, finally knocking on his door, where Vicente at last greeted him with a steely, flat expression.

"Really?" Vicente mumbled, giving him a second to feel ashamed before returning to the couch. He stretched his long arms over his head with a yawn.

Alex spied the empty wine bottle in front of him. "Seriously? You finished the whole thing?"

"You've been gone more than an hour."

"I… I haven't."

"Oh, but you have. Look." Vicente nodded at the old-fashioned clock Alex had kept with him since first leaving home. Its hands betrayed him, reading 12.55 a.m.

"I'm sorry. It honestly didn't feel…"

Vicente drained the last of the wine in his glass, setting it down so hard on the coffee table. Alex was relieved it didn't crack.

Alex flopped down in the couch next to him, wiping the sweat from his palms on his trousers. "He's an interesting guy."

"I didn't ask. You got anything else to drink?"

He rolled his eyes. One of those nights, he did not need. "You haven't had enough?"

Vicente made an exaggerated groan and lay his head in Alex's lap. "Whoever said being poor had some kind of nobility to it was full of bullshit."

"Yeah," Alex laughed, gently stroking Vicente's sandy hair. "Who was it who said that?"

"Arsehole."

"Wanker."

"Bastard."

"Fascist."

"Oh, definitely a Fascist!"

Alex paused his touch, letting his fingertips rest on Vicente's cheek. Vicente brought a hand up and clasped his fingers. "You really think this guy can help?"

"This guy? It's our show, Vis."

"Right, so he's not a distraction? He's not changing the way you're looking at it just a bit?"

"Look, what is this about? You can't be jealous."

"Can't I?" Vicente sat up, smoothed his hair, and eyed Alex with curiosity. Then without warning, he leaned forward and kissed him full on the mouth.

Alex accepted his tongue without thinking, then pushed him away. "What is with you tonight?"

Vicente shrugged and got to his feet. "Don't tell me you're not distracted."

"Vis, what the fuck?" Alex nursed his lip as if Vicente had hit him. "Joanna—"

"Don't fucking hide behind Joanna, man. She's not what's going on here. I'll see you tomorrow."

Without another word, Vicente gathered up his kit bag and left, letting the door slam behind him. A dog in one of the nearby apartments started barking. Alex sat on the couch, staring at the empty wine bottle. Piece by piece, ideas began to come, and he began to write.

CHAPTER FIVE

"What?"

"*What?*"

"Fuck that!"

"Talking like that will not change anything," said Maria, lifting her glasses from her nose with a sigh. "It's about sales. You haven't made them. Nobody is talking about your show. No press. Nothing. I can offer you the theatre for a week in February, but for now, I need a sure thing."

"Maria, this isn't right. We have a deal."

"A deal? Two weeks theatre rental paid with profit share? Sounds like an okay deal for you, at least if there is a profit, which there isn't. Check your contract. A profit-share rental can be bumped or moved for any operational reason at the discretion of the management, and that's me. You should be thanking me. At least this way you have six months to get off your arses and start building a crowd. I don't know what you thought was going to happen. That I was going to promote it for you, perhaps? Like I don't have enough to do."

"Maria, please, we're about to completely change the show. Just give us one rehearsal, then come to the next one. You'll see how great this is going to—"

"Wait, wait…" She silenced Alex with a wave. "You're *completely* changing the show?"

Alex's heart sank as he recognised his tactical error.

"That's probably for the best. From what I saw…" Maria's shrug hit Alex like a kick to the gut. "But if you're changing so much, February would be much better, yes? It's settled then."

"Maria, please. It won't take us—"

"Will you stop? I've already filled your slot and the first week is three-quarters sold. Come back when you can turn numbers like that."

Vicente shook his head. "You already… who?"

Maria shrugged again. "Someone called Si-Man."

"Si-Man?"

"Yes, as in 'See'-Man."

Alex bit his tongue. This was already ludicrous enough.

"And what does Si-Man do?" asked Joanna, who until now had remained quiet behind her fake, frozen smile.

"Sell tickets. Beyond that, I don't care."

"And are we talking about a singer? A dancer? A performance artist? A clown? Just who the hell is this person?"

"By all the saints." Maria snatched a flyer from her desk and passed it to Alex. He hoped the picture that resembled a gigantic, angry mutant baby with a Sonny Bono wig, dark tufts of hastily trimmed chest hair and a green-painted moustache wasn't the artist. "Do you know how much crap goes up on that stage? I don't ask why. I just count the receipts."

There wasn't much text to go on. Just a venue and a date… that evening.

"We should go," Joanna said.

"What?"

"What?"

"If it's selling already based on this truly hideous flyer that explains nothing, I want to know why, don't you?"

"Grand idea," said Maria, putting her glasses back on. "I don't know what the hell he's doing, but you should be taking notes."

"You're not seriously saying we should buy tickets for this?"

"Buy them?" Joanna scoffed. "Surely between the two of you, someone owes you a favour or really enjoyed the sex."

"If I get you comps, will it get you out of my office?" asked Maria. "Because I can't spend all day arguing about this. Listen, I like you three, but you need to smarten up about how this all works. Right now, every young person in Madrid who's put every substance into their damn body and had every insane idea in between fucking everything that moves from the Retiro to de Campo now thinks they're an artist. I just know I need to keep the lights on and eat. Are we understood?"

Alex, Joanna and Vicente stared back at her in stunned silence.

"Out," she said quietly.

They were too dumbstruck to argue.

*　　*　　*

"My arse will swallow the sins of men until I barf oceans of rage that will punish the sleeping sycophants of the old order."

This was the line that lost Alex, and had it not come just ten minutes into what Si-Man and his audience were calling a show, he might have walked out. Joanna, ever perceptive, had put one hand on his knee and the other on Vicente's, a private gesture they'd adopted, assuring each other that somehow, they would endure the next fifty minutes together and laugh about it afterwards, no matter how wretchedly drunk they needed to get. It seemed to work. They'd not yet snuck out on a show, which seemed almost impossible in this tiny space. Alex also had a feeling it would earn them jeers from the crowd, as if they'd blasphemed the diaper-clad messiah who'd just fished half a tomato from said diaper and begun rubbing it up and down his body like it was a giant, living piece of breakfast toast.

He jumped as Si-Man let out a primal scream that rattled the flimsy backdrop. Several audience members gasped with anticipation of what would come, which turned out to be several violent exhales followed by a swooping, bowing gesture. Si-Man then lifted his head, facing the crowd with lips pursed and extended like a baboon. He rubbed the tomato over his face before throwing it to the stage with a loud splat. He then pulled back the skin around his eyes, reducing them to slits like some racist Jerry Lewis character before banging on his chest and leading the audience in a chant about "*seeing through their lies.*" As most of the audience shouted along, the show began to take on the tone of a strange political rally crossed with an American gospel revival, as Si-Man alternated between stomping around in a circle and wiggling his arse at the crowd.

Alex could see Maria's face now.

"*Covered in shit, covered in shit, covered in shit...*" sang Si-Man while slapping himself on the backside, doing a jig onstage. The chant continued, a ghoulish whisper that quickly surrounded the three of them as the crowd took it up. Vicente stifled a laugh, which was thankfully lost under the incantation.

Si-Man lifted a small notebook from the pocket of his filthy jacket and read not three, or five, but eight short poems, each less comprehensible and more self-indulgent than the last. Alex tuned out until the next chant began, "*I am Maya! I am Inca! I am the Philippines!*"

"Oh shit, we're going here?" Vicente said under his breath.

"*A voice for the voiceless!*"

"I feel like I've fallen into a Dali painting," Alex murmured. "Only it sucks."

His neighbour shushed him loudly, a sound quickly buried under another primal scream as Si-Man began pummelling the stage with his fists. He then spread his fingers in a diamond shape and pretended to fuck the gap inside it, ranting something about *"restoring the lives they stole. We hear you great thinkers and spirits of lost lands. We see the sins of our vile fathers and are not like them!"*

Smallpox and genocide, yes, but to Alex's knowledge, at least the conquistadors had never subjected their victims to a show like this.

"This, is our great healing. Together as one heart and spirit."

"Oh, good Lord…"

"Shhhhhhhh!!!"

"As avatars of the Great Montezuma—"

Alex could stand no more. Ignoring the looks and indignant grunts from those he passed, he edged his way over several sets of knees to the end of the row and snuck out as quietly as he could.

"Yea, know we cannot walk from this, brother!"

Alex hurriedly shut the door behind him, expelling his relief in one long, steady breath.

*   *   *

"Alex?" Leo said. "I thought that was you. What did you think of the show?"

As if his night could get any worse. Alex hoped the third glass of wine he now held would kick in soon. "It was… a show."

"He's brilliant, isn't he? Completely shakes off the conventions of structure and dramaturgy—"

"He certainly does that."

"—while delivering a message that feels so today. As we shake off the shackles, what about the shackles we left behind? Ooof! It gives me chills."

"We? Who is 'we,' Leo? And who's doing the shaking? Because Semen—"

"Si-Man."

"*Si-Man*, seemed to think he was single-handedly saving the colonised world. It was patronising, Leo. It was gross and borderline racist."

Leo let out an exaggerated sigh. "Not everyone can get it, I suppose."

"I suppose not. Now excuse me, I think I see someone—"

"Oh, you know someone here? Wouldn't think it's your crowd. Who?"

"Anybody."

"What?"

"Antonio. Yes, I think that's him. Excuse me." Alex ducked away toward the stranger he'd picked to be his hastily invented friend. In the corner, he spied Vicente nursing a bottle of beer while he waited for Joanna.

"Are you okay?" Vicente asked.

Alex shook his head. "I think I'm actually dumber after watching that. I'll let you know later if I remember how to put on pants."

"Maybe we should ditch *Blood Wedding* and do *The Emperor's New Clothes*?"

"He was wearing a diaper."

"Right. Apparently ready to be covered in—"

"There you are!" Joanna swept toward them with a bored-looking woman sporting thick spectacles and a bob haircut. "This is Peach. She's kindly offered to introduce us to Si-Man."

"Pardon?"

"Introduce us?" asked Alex. "That's really not necessary."

"Chill, brother." Peach's tone contradicted her stiff smile. "Joanna tells me you guys bumped your slot so we could have a two-week run. Right on. I know Si-Man is way grateful. The least we can do to give back is share the energy, you know?"

"You're his manager?"

"Woah, woah, harsh word. My name's Peach, and it's my job to reach opportunities. Inspiration. I'm Si-Man's arms, mind, and heart. Holding them together those times when the world is just too much. We all need a little help holding on, you know?"

"He does seem a sensitive soul."

"Oh man, you've just seen the surface. Just the *sur-face*. Come see the show we've got planned for your old slot."

"Will there be quite so much bare arse?" Vicente asked.

"Hey!"

With a wave from Peach, the artist was present. Joanna switched from Peach's arm to Vicente's, as Alex reflexively extended a hand. Before Peach had even introduced them, Si-Man had grasped Alex behind both ears and brought their foreheads together until they were gently touching. He smelled like rancid tomato. He then did the same to Joanna. Vicente demurred, which earned him a look of disgust from Peach.

"Thank you, thank you my friends. It means the world to me that you…" Si-Man's gaze landed on Alex as if seeing him for the first time. "You walked out."

"I was overcome. The part about us all being connected to the empires our ancestors destroyed. Wow, man. Just wow."

"Right on." Si-Man adjusted his diaper. "I mean every word. The stage is a sacred space, you know? We can't pollute it with lies, or it, in turn, pollutes our souls. Cinema is a perversion built on lies. We must preserve the sacred stage space."

Right, thought Alex. Less artist, more cult leader, then?

"Peach tells me you're the show that bailed for us? Truly, man—"

"Oh, it was nothing," Alex answered, playing along. When the interruption seemed to annoy Si-Man, he shut up.

"Not nothing, my friend, it was a sign. A sure sign to me that you three understand the sacred nature of art, and that the stage can't be polluted with something unready. Many artists don't get that, brother. You have my gratitude and my respect."

"I… that wasn't quite—"

"We just want to put on something great," Joanna jumped in.

"That you will. Your energy is…" Si-Man licked his lips as he approached her. "…ancient. Yet you're so now."

"They're so, *so* now, Si-Man."

Alex had forgotten Peach was there. He was too busy watching Vicente's face to see if it would crack as Si-Man put his hand on Joanna's. Damn. Maybe Vicente should have been an actor.

"You've been stealing?" Si-Man took a gold-painted ping-pong ball from Joanna's hand.

"You gifted it to me." She turned to Alex. "This was after you left."

"I got that," he answered.

"The gift is my show. In it, I give everything I have." Si-Man smiled at Alex. "Think you can do that? What is your little show about, anyhow?"

If Vicente wanted to hit the man now, Alex would have let him. Several of Si-Man's faithful came to his rescue just in time, pulling the artist away without so much as a goodbye from him or Peach. Joanna pocketed the ball once more. With no more than a look between them, they knew it was time to leave.

Vicente grabbed a bottle of red wine from an unattended table they passed. "He just accused us of stealing? Okay, then."

The dry, warm air of the summer night wrapped around them, and to the left, a glowing cigarette revealed the face of Jago, who grinned as they joined him. He offered up a cigarette, which Vicente declined, though Alex could tell he was itching for one.

"What did you think?" Jago asked.

It should have surprised him that Jago was here, but it didn't. Just as it hadn't surprised him when he'd turned up at the café.

"It was… interesting," Joanna conceded.

A few seconds of silence passed before the four of them erupted into laugher—even Vicente.

"Except now, he's got our slot," Alex said.

"I'm sorry?" Jago asked, his eyes widening. "I thought you were opening in two weeks?"

"So did we. Apparently, Maria needs surefire sales, which she's somehow getting from…" Alex tossed his head in the direction of the doors. "…that."

"Oof! No accounting for fashion, I suppose. That would explain why I didn't see you all at the Culture Forum this afternoon."

"Oh, shit!" Alex cringed. "Sorry. We didn't know how to reach—"

"It's fine. It's an interesting place to explore," said Jago, easing himself off the wall. "Come on. I want to share something with the three of you."

*　*　*

They followed Calle de Atocha down to the wide avenue that was Paseo del Prado, rounding the enormous art museum to the locked gates of the Retiro Park.

"So much for a late-night stroll," Vicente said.

"Trust me."

Within a minute, Jago had disappeared beneath some shrubbery. His head popped out again as he beckoned for them to follow. A short scramble and several scratches later, they stumbled out onto the broad walkways of a dark and silent Retiro.

"It's not dangerous?" Alex had heard stories of what happened to guys who roamed the parks at night.

"Not with four of us," Jago answered with a mischievous grin.

"Don't be a spoilsport, Alex," said Joanna, following Jago in earnest.

They stopped at the enormous fountain of the fallen angel. To Alex's knowledge, it was the only monument to Lucifer in existence, at least, in a space so public and obvious as the Retiro. He was amazed the Fascists and their church cronies hadn't torn it down. Though the fountain's waters were still, the face of the Morningstar was clearly illuminated in the cloudless night, as was the phalanx of loyal demons at his feet, each warning would-be climbers away with its own infernal little scowl.

"What shall we drink to?" Jago asked, nodding at the wine in Vicente's hand. "To certain performance artists' careers? May they shine brightly but briefly."

"Cruel," Joanna admonished him, as Vicente opened the wine and passed it over. "But fair."

Jago took a swig of the wine, then passed it to Joanna, who passed it to Alex. Vicente declined.

"Come on, darling," Joanna said with gentle mockery. "This is your loot."

"And it's incredibly bad luck to break a drinking circle," added Jago. "At least in Peru or… somewhere. We are all one spirit tonight, aren't we?"

Vicente forced a smile and took his drink.

"Do you often come down here?" Alex asked.

"Seldom. It seemed an occasion best enjoyed with new friends."

"You knew a gap in the fence."

"They can't wall off the whole thing, can they?" Jago turned, admiring Lucifer's expression. "Just five outcasts thrown together."

"You think so?"

Jago smiled at Vicente, taking another drink and starting a new round. "Did you or did you not just lose your theatre and rehearsal space?"

"Yeah, we did. To that…" Vicente growled when words failed him. "February, man. We're supposed to wait until February?"

"I imagine you could put together quite the show by then. Of course, there is such a thing as too much rehearsal." Jago turned to stare at Joanna, saying nothing at first, until… "Will you show us?"

Joanna shook her head. "Show you what?"

"What you've worked on. You've been dying to all evening. I can see that particular glint in your eye, like you're excited to share a discovery but you're afraid that if it's left too long, you'll seem foolish. So don't leave it. Show us."

"Now, you mean?"

Alex was just as hesitant. "Jago, I think—"

"Mister Si-Man calls the stage a sacred space." Jago raised a hand toward the fallen Morningstar. "In the absence of a stage, I am asking you to dance for the profane."

Alex, Joanna, and Vicente exchanged looks, but… why not? Joanna knew the music as well as if it had been pressed to a record inside her head. Her gaze landed on Alex, who acquiesced with a silent nod.

As her audience of three—four if they counted the Morningstar—took their seats on the fountain's edge, Joanna began moving through ten minutes of completely new steps. The violence, the hunger, the love and fear… it was all there, but gone were the barriers of the text itself. It was something new, vibrant and frightening, yet just as delightful. Alex felt as if each movement were nourishing his mind and soul after the exhaustion that had been Si-Man's self-aggrandised salvation. When the dance was done, they sat silently in Lucifer's shadow, watching Joanna scratch at the ground beneath her feet. At last, she rose with movements as slow as nature would allow.

A shiver swept through Alex, as if February had arrived already and caught them with its sudden, bitter kiss. "Brava," he said at last, just loud enough for her to hear.

Joanna pulled her dark hair off her face, tying it back as it had been before her dance. "It's getting there."

"Jo?" added Vicente. "That was incredible."

"Thank you, darling. You're very sweet."

"I mean it. You were great before, but this is something—"

"Vicente," said Jago. "She knows."

Vicente resisted biting that, much to Alex's relief. Still, he wasn't so sure Joanna did know. By the dance's end, she'd seemed uncertain, even frustrated. He'd seen it in her eyes, just for an instant, as if she'd come so close to the perfection she sought, only to have it snatched away in one final moment, lost to silence.

"Vis?" she said. "I'm tired."

"I'm not surprised." He got up and took her in a hug. "You were up rehearsing most of last night."

"Take me home?"

It lasted only a second, but Alex caught the sceptical look Vicente gave him. He had played nice all evening, but that look conveyed just one idea—Jago.

"Go," Alex said softly but firmly. "We'll be fine."

"You're sure?"

"Yes."

"Can you find your way back to the gap in the fence?" asked Jago.

Joanna was already there, pulling back the shrubs to reveal the broken links. "Goodnight, boys!"

Vicente shook his head, taking Alex in a hug before reluctantly accepting a much shorter one from Jago, who gave him back the wine. "Goodnight."

"Vicente," Jago said after they parted. "Everything's going to be fine."

After so many forced smiles, Alex had to wonder if Vicente would need the rest more than Joanna. He sat, left in comfortable silence with Jago, who dragged his hand through the waters of the fountain. Alex reached out and began doing the same. The water felt surprisingly cool, refreshing him as he rubbed some of it on his forearms, face, and neck.

"Don't drink any," Jago cautioned him. "I can't say with any certainty that someone hasn't pissed in this."

"Hah. You're joking. Wait, are you? Or is this your way of telling me you need a leak?"

Jago smiled, taking a golden ping-pong ball from his pocket. He began tossing it in the air, catching it each time with clockwork regularity.

"Did Joanna give you that?"

"The idiot launched about five of these into the audience like it was a Thai sex show."

"Launched them from what?"

"Best not ask those sorts of questions, Alex."

"Noted. You don't mind if I insist on you washing your hands when you're done?

Jago laughed, tossing the ping-pong ball away into the water. "We live in a city awash with artists, most of them not very good. But this has been true for the entirety of human endeavour. So what? I'm not saying they shouldn't try."

"What are you saying?" In Alex's brief experience, Jago had not been shy of sharing his opinion.

They spied the beams of two flashlights in a far corner of the park.

"Maybe we should go home," Alex suggested, noticing his leg resting against Jago's.

"You mean to our respective homes, of course? Like the respectable, upstanding young men we are?"

They got to their feet, each admiring the playful glint in the other's eye.

"No," said Alex. "I mean to mine."

Jago regarded him with an inviting smile. "I think mine is closer, yes? And larger? And there's something I wish to give you, if that's all right."

Alex was too curious to say no.

CHAPTER SIX

"You moved to Madrid two years ago?"

"Mmhmm." Jago took another pull from his beer and sank further into the orange couch.

"From Andalusia?"

"No, from Mexico, and Colombia before that."

"Shit." Alex sipped more of his drink. He could only imagine such travels. "I've never left Spain."

"Never?"

"Does Barcelona count?"

"That very much depends on who you ask," Jago said, raising his beer. "We are a country cobbled together by history and coincidence. The Basques, the Galicians, the Andalusians, the Catalonians… How did you meet Joanna?"

Alex had learned during their conversation that such an abrupt change of subject was not unusual for Jago, but it still threw him off-guard. "Through Vicente."

"Ah, and he is your ex-boyfriend? Funny. It so often goes the other way. Girls first."

"He's bisexual."

"I never said he wasn't. It was just an observation. He protects you like a Golden Retriever."

Alex didn't know enough about dogs to answer that. "I wish he'd focus more on protecting Joanna."

"I think she's more likely to protect him, no?" Jago corrected Alex with a confidence that bemused him. "She is a remarkable individual."

"You mean her dancing?"

"I mean everything."

"You're not attracted—"

"Oh gods, no. To her talent, sure, and to her energy. But no, she doesn't speak to my dick, if that's what you're asking."

Alex smiled. "You have a very forthright way of speaking, you know that?"

"And would you prefer I was vague? Spoke in platitudes? The show tonight was crap, and if Si-Man and his orbiting lapdog, Apricot—"

"Peach. Her name was Peach."

"Whatever. If they'd asked me, I would have told them so. After all his ranting about honesty on stage, we'd see how much honesty he could really take."

"You've got a mean side too."

Jago's eyes widened with mock offence. "I just don't like my time being wasted."

"Then why go? I mean, you seem to know your shit when it comes to theatre. Surely, you didn't think it was going to be good?"

"It was not him I came to see."

Alex paused before taking another drink. "Wait, you don't mean me?"

"Why not you?"

"How did you even know we'd be there?"

Jago got up, returning to the couch with a small deck of oversized cards. "You're familiar with the tarot?"

"Wait, wait, wait. You're telling me some cards told you where we'd be?"

"Nothing so specific." Jago shuffled the cards quickly, held them close to the centre of his chest for a moment, then cut them before drawing the top three and laying them out on the coffee table. Cards called the Tower and Death faced them, with a Four of Wands upside down in between.

"That doesn't look good."

"Again, you're being too literal. The Tower can mean revolution or upheaval, usually painful, yes. But here, it's in your past. Something you've worked through. A shedding of painful family bonds, perhaps?"

Alex bit his lip, not ready to answer that.

Jago shrugged. "It might also be something on a larger scale. Perhaps even the dictatorship, though that seems a lazy reach. As I said, it's in the past. The card in the middle signifies where you are, while the one on the right—"

"Death? Death's my future?"

"Death is everybody's future. But in the tarot, it usually means a transition or evolution, often a positive one. A nice card to get in that slot, if I may say so. But in the middle here…" He tapped the edge of the Four of Wands. "…this is a more personal source of pain."

Alex was intrigued. "Personal?"

"Safety? Security? Family? Purpose? Belonging? These are things belonging to the Four of Wands, but in your case, as the card of your present, it's inverted."

"Meaning I don't have those things?"

"Or you feel you don't, but under all of that… self-doubt, perhaps?"

Alex smiled, shaking his head. "Now you're just telling me what I already know."

"That's the point. The cards are signposts. They help you find the answers you already possess, even if you've dismissed or buried them. They're not oracles. They might teach you to trust a good feeling as much as a good idea, like your dance show. You understand now?"

"You mean it's interpretation?"

"It's a conversation, and the message changes with each person who sees it. I mean, unless you're someone like Si-Man who wants everyone to share his own vision and experience because it's so fucking compelling."

"Let's maybe let that one go," Alex suggested with a smile.

"Gladly. Would you like another beer?"

"No, I'm okay. Thanks." He shivered as Jago stroked his fingertips on the back of the couch. "I should go."

"Why?"

"I just… I want to focus on the show right now."

Jago lifted his chin, sinking dejectedly into the couch. "You're not going to show your audience anything honest if you start by lying to me."

"I'm not lying. I want the show to be…" He allowed the words to float into nothingness, instead resuming the conversation he'd wanted to finish with Jago outside the Teatro Español. One no less expressive for its lack of words. Bloody hell, Jago knew how to kiss. Even after the beers, his lips were sweet with red wine and the soft flesh of his hands as they brushed Alex's temples made him shiver.

"I trust your ability to multitask." Jago caught Alex's lips with his once more in a way that made Alex only want to hold Jago close and kiss him for as long as breath would allow. He smelled like the sun; like home, only Jago tasted like the man Alex wished he'd been at home but never could. When they finally broke, Jago smiled with uncharacteristic shyness. "What's wrong?"

"Nothing. I just don't want to rush things."

"Things?"

Jago's smile widened. "Going to make me work for it, aren't you? Bitch."

"Work for what?"

Jago tilted his head, staring at Alex as if he were a puzzle in need of solving. True, he was playing up the obtuse act with insufferable cuteness, but only because he was trying to avoid the lingering question that thickened the sexual energy between them.

"I want to give you a massage."

Alex blinked twice. This was not the offer he'd expected. "You mean, like…"

"My hands on you, pressing your skin, working out knots in your muscles and hopefully relaxing you. Yes, that's what I mean. Is that okay?"

"I… I suppose."

"You've never had one, have you?"

Alex shook his head, his naivety no longer an act. The playful glint returned to Jago's eye as he got up from the couch, crossed to the hidden door on which Alex had intruded, pressed it into the wall to open it, and beckoned Alex inside.

"You're sure?" Alex asked. "You seemed pretty adamant last time."

"Get in here before I change my mind," Jago purred.

The door shut behind them, plunging the room into darkness. Yet no sooner had it clicked shut than the walls took on a luminescence of their own, glowing with gentle, warm orange light, which crept across them like a rapidly growing vine. Alex watched in awe as the light created by this effect wrapped itself around the room, lightening the space around Jago's desk, and beyond it, a red and black carpet surrounded by pillows. The books, the skull, the birds, the symbols… every piece he'd seen on his last visit remained in place, but the warm light made this seem like the domain of a scholar, not someone embarrassed about his strange hobbies.

"I'm sorry, I lied to you earlier." Jago pushed his chair beneath the desk, removed his belt and trousers, and kneeled down on the carpet. He peeled off his socks before unbuttoning his shirt. "I mean, I have done taxidermy, but just the once. This room? It's my sacred space and sanctuary. I wasn't ready to share that with you yet. I hope you understand." He extended a hand toward Alex, who approached with far more caution.

"Are you sure?" Alex asked. "I don't want to intrude."

"Stop being so damned English."

"There's no need to be rude."

"You're here because I desire it, and I hope you do too. The type of massage I do is a sacred interaction, not just between bodies but between souls. I like you, Alex. I'm not only ready to show you this room, I'm ready to share it with you. Do you understand the difference?"

Alex shuffled his feet. "You *are* gay, right?"

"Yes."

"So you mean sex?"

For an instant, Jago looked offended. "We'll see. First, your clothes, please. There should be no barriers between us." He peeled off his shirt and tossed it on one of the pillows at the side of the room. For the first time, Alex saw the muscular contours of Jago's compact body. These extended to a sharp v-cut, which disappeared into a dark thatch of public hair framing a modest but well-formed cock.

Alex wondered if Jago always forewent underwear, or if the move was choreographed.

Jago eased his body forward, extending it like a snake as he pulled himself on his hands towards Alex, tightening the muscles of his lightly furred and perfectly rounded behind as he turned it to the ceiling with a grin. "Don't make me come up there."

Alex quickly opened his belt and shucked off his trousers, followed by his socks.

Jago rolled over, his cock lolling to one side as he rested both hands beneath his head, watching Alex disrobe with a patient smile.

Alex paused before taking off his shirt, only continuing when a nod from Jago boosted his confidence. He felt silly, being so self-conscious in front of a man dressed as nature made him, but touching the soft paunch of his belly, he was suddenly aware of the untrimmed pubes that would accentuate the so-so-dimensions of his cock, the annoying tufts of hair that had begun to sprout on his back, the ugly scar on his right flank, and the one front tooth slightly longer than the other.

"You really hate being on stage, don't you?"

Jago asked this with such tenderness that Alex managed to dismiss his doubts long enough to toss away his clothes and stand naked before his host.

"Very nice," Jago breathed, gently wetting his lips as he extended a hand.

It was an unapologetically lustful gesture, and it hadn't been forced. What this man saw in him, Alex couldn't say, but if he didn't stop searching for it, it would deny him the moment he'd craved with Jago since their first conversation outside the cinema.

"Thanks," he said, lowering to his knees.

Jago reached out and stroked his cheek. "Now, lie down on your stomach."

"Sorry?"

"Did you think the massage was just a pretext?" Jago reached for a small pot of creamy ointment on a low shelf just beyond where they sat.

Alex did his best to dismiss the faint stirring this set off in his— *lack* of pants—and there he was, standing at attention for all to see. But if Jago noticed, he didn't draw attention to it. Alex quickly rolled over, doing his best to smother the fleshy traitor and get comfortable.

"Just lie in whatever position makes you comfortable. Don't try and anticipate me, just enjoy it."

Anticipation? That was one word for it. He'd expected the ointment to be cooler for some reason, but as Jago's hand wrapped around the middle of his left leg, working the stuff in with smooth, upwards gliding motions that teased the crease of his butt before being repeated, Alex found it impossible to do anything but comply. Each stroke was methodical, as if Jago had spent impossible years studying the craft.

"Remember to breathe," he purred, hands reaching the curve of Alex's shoulder blade.

"Where did you learn this?" He heard a light, playful sigh, as if Jago had started to laugh but had not wanted to make him feel foolish. He gasped as he felt Jago's knee slide into the gap between his thighs, just as he pushed his hands along Alex's back once more, making sure to cover every inch of skin.

"You're so jumpy," Jago said. It didn't bother Alex so much that Jago had avoided his question, not when he swooped down and kissed the back of Alex's ear. "You have a lovely body, Alex. It's earthy, natural, and human."

Alex couldn't help but tense again, which earned him a playful slap on the rear.

"I won't harp on it if it makes you uncomfortable, but I do think you need to be told, now and again." Jago rested his hands on the small of Alex's back for a second. "You seriously never thought someone would?"

The question caught Alex by such complete surprise, he barely noticed the massage continue, or Jago pressing harder, slipping his hands down both flanks. "I don't know that I *never* thought that."

"There's nothing wrong with having fears. Some would say it's crucial. The fear of never being loved? Never being desired? Feeling like your creativity and vision isn't wanted, even in a city that seems open to everything? Rejection is a universal fear."

Alex winced as Jago pressed into the soles of his feet. At least the pain took away any tickling sensation. "How do you know that?"

"Because I've never known a creative who doesn't feel it. Then, along come the cackling cynics and sycophants. Like flies they attach themselves to whoever they think is the hippest big thing, but they buzz away again just as soon as they get bored or feel threatened, since they may be the only creatures on earth less secure than the artists they haunt. Don't change your flavour for them. The last thing you need to become is another Si-Man. Turn over."

"Already?"

"I want to see your eyes."

Alex did as he was told, silently trying to read what Jago was thinking inside that enviably curious brain. Alex wrinkled his face in confusion as Jago eased himself forward, lifting Alex's leg and placing it over his shoulder while he applied more of the ointment to the front of Alex's thighs. It seemed so absurdly intimate, yet it felt good, having Jago pressing into him, sliding his hands toward where their cocks now warmed one another. He might have been at least semi-erect if Jago weren't pressing so damn hard into the muscles of his leg. Alex groaned, breathing through the pain.

"Not big on hamstring stretches, are we?" Jago teased, pausing to let Alex catch his breath before he continued.

"Hey, not all of us were raised by athletes as some are raised by wolves."

Jago laughed at that. "Flatterer. Good genes and sit-ups."

"Sit-ups? I thought it was—"

"You do realise I'm feeling just a touch objectified right now?"

"Sor—*Ow!*" Alex started as Jago squeezed a point high on the inside of his leg.

"Sorry," they said together, before laughing again.

"I just haven't known many artsy folk who are so…" Alex searched for a word that *wouldn't* make his host feel objectified. "You know, other than dancers."

"Yes, well, your Joanna and I share some interests. But it's as I told you. I am the person I am. Where possible, I've put time and energy into becoming the person I wish to be. I don't know what else to tell you."

"You don't have to tell me anything. Sorry, I don't mean to… just drop it."

"I will, *after* I thank you for the compliment." Jago shifted his weight, lowered Alex's leg and picked up the other one, assuming the same position on the other side.

"What brought you to the movie the other night?" Alex asked, eager to switch the subject as easily as they'd switched legs.

"Didn't I tell you? I've seen the director's band, and his drag. I liked both. Why should I not see his movie?"

"It was pretty great, huh?"

"No."

"Hmm?"

"It was good, but not great. He'll make much greater, I promise you."

"You seem very sure of that." Alex winced with pain, prompting Jago to pause again.

"He is that rarest of people who despite all their fears of rejection, somehow catch lightning in a bottle. Lorca had that. Cervantes had it. Goya and Velazquez had it." A sneer cross Jago's face. "Buñuel and Dali had it, though what they've done with it since… Christ!"

"You're not a Dali fan, I take it?"

"I was once. Of Buñuel too, but Bunuel is a pompous arse and a subtle bigot beneath all his noble bluster, while Salvad…" Jago trailed off, setting Alex's leg down again and applying more of the ointment to Alex's lower legs and feet before repositioning himself to work Alex's shoulders. "It doesn't matter. The world loves them now."

"If you're about to tell me that you and Dali are on a first-name basis, I'll believe it."

Jago suppressed a laugh, slipping his hands across the curves of Alex's collarbone until he began working the muscle of his outer chest. "Did you know they made a film about Lorca? The two of them, I mean, Buñuel and Dali."

"You mean a documentary?"

"No. A short horror film. Experimental, I suppose you'd call it. It was not very flattering."

"No? I thought they were friends."

"You don't name a work *Un Chien Andalou* in honour of a man you call a friend."

Alex's French was rusty, but it was close enough to the Spanish that he understood. "An Andalusian Dog?"

Jago nodded solemnly as he finished up his steady sweeps on Alex's chest and turned his attention to his arms. "Can you imagine calling him a dog? A provincial poser, fresh off the farm? They denied it, of course; dismissed it as a silly joke, but the title has nothing to do with the film, so there's little one can say to defend them. You've noticed it, I'm sure."

"Noticed what?"

"The way some of them talk to you… or don't. How nice it is that you, a farm boy, want to be creative while the hipper-than-thou continually ignore you or treat your work as something to suffer through or worse, ignore? The gatekeeping by these self-appointed taste-makers?" Jago made a retching sound. "Thankfully, they're a minority. Most people want to see you succeed for no other reason than they like good shows. You just need some of *your* people to notice you. The others will follow. That's why you should have said hello to him the other night."

"To the director? I wouldn't know what to say."

"Tell him you liked the film. My god, it's praise. It doesn't have to be original, just genuine. The second you start posing, then you become a poser."

"I suppose so." Alex moaned with satisfaction as Jago took hold of his hand and worked the ointment into the spaces between his fingers. "But what's that got to do with Lorca? An Andalusian Dog?"

"Because it can take hundreds and hundreds of compliments to build us up and one shitty act of spite to destroy us. Just one nasty bitch, eagerly awaiting a failure. Or one who wants to make a movie mocking you."

"You're sure that wasn't just spite from a bitter ex? You said Dali and Lorca—"

"I suppose that's possible. All this to say, I understand your anxiety. How it's paralysed your show. But it will get better, I promise you. Joanna doesn't suffer the same fears. Strange, in that way, among others. It's like she's an older soul."

"Umm… thanks, I think?"

"Would I be here now, with you, if I was lying? Listen, my little bundle of high tension and insecurity, you belong here. You've every right to do this work and have it seen, and don't let anyone tell you differently." Jago smeared a little more of the ointment onto Alex's face. Alex sighed with pleasure as Jago slid his hands down the length of his body one last time, slipping them between Alex's thighs and smearing his now unapologetically attentive genitals with the ointment. "In the words of the cunning Shylock, 'since I am a dog, beware my fangs.'"

Alex opened his eyes to see the Jago grinning in all toothy glory as his dark, handsome features hovered above him. "To the dogs of Andalusia."

"To all of us Andalusia dogs." Jago gave him a quick, wet lick on the nose. "Woof."

"Woof," Alex replied, now grinning too. "Woof, woof."

Jago began panting, his tongue outstretched in self-mockery before easing back on his haunches and howling as if the moon itself could hear. Alex pushed himself up, and sitting across from Jago, began to howl too.

"Awwooooooo!" Jago howled with a laugh. "*Awwoooooooooo!!!!!*"

Alex's howl collapsed into laughter. "We won't bother your neighbours?"

"Not from in here." Jago said, arms outstretched as he caught his breath. "My sacred place, remember? How are you feeling?"

"Amazing. I don't know what you were doing or where you learned it, but…" A few more seconds passed between them, and for the first time since Jago had asked him to lie down, Alex felt awkward. "I should probably go."

"Perhaps, but I hope you won't."

It occurred to Alex as their lips met that he'd not kissed a man like this in a long time; with earnestness and courage, yet also a tentativeness that came from wanting the kiss to deepen with each passing second. Their shared nudity had stripped away much of his nervousness, and what remained made the taste of Jago one he longed to intensify. Jago, who up until now had been so in control of their time together, from the beer, to the massage, to even leading their questions, now lay on his back, his smile one of gentle adoration as he stroked Alex's cheek. Torn between the urge to kiss him again and hover above him, drinking in every second of that smile, Alex let out a nervous giggle.

"What?" Jago said.

"I just wasn't expecting this. You're more beautiful than I thought."

"I'm not sure how to take that."

"I mean—I'll shut up. I know you have guys telling you you're beautiful all the time."

Jago cupped his hand around Alex's jaw, stroking the curve of his ear with a stray fingertip. "Not guys I care to hear it from, usually. There comes a time when casual sex starts to burn you out."

Alex took Jago's hand in his and kissed it impulsively. "Can't say I've yet had that particular burnout."

"It will happen. You stay in Madrid long enough? Or Barcelona or Mexico City... even New York or London. Anywhere that gathers men like us. It makes me fearful, sometimes. Such great hedonistic parties throughout history have seldom fizzled out. They're more often crushed by an unwelcome visitor. The church. The Fascists. The plague..." He shook his head vehemently. "Gosh, I sound cheery."

Alex tried to brush his dire prediction off with a shrug. "You certainly have a dark side."

"You worked that out so quickly?"

Feeling emboldened, Alex began stroking the contours of Jago's chest. "Did we or did we not dance in the shadow of the devil's image tonight?"

Jago laughed, pulling Alex closer and wrapping him in a warm hug, accompanied by another deep, welcome kiss. It had occurred to Alex at some point during the massage how cool the room was, at least relative to outside, or even compared to the rest of the apartment. But reasoning this seemed a waste of time with Jago's naked body pinned against his. He brought his knee up between Jago's legs, pressing their bodies into each other with renewed hunger until their kiss broke again.

"Perhaps that's why all that sex with those tourist boys—Americans, English, and French guys, Germans—leaves me cold. I'm a secret Cassandra." Jago mocked his own sentence with wide eyes as he stroked Alex's hair. "Beware, beware!"

"Our Sister Cassandra of the Immaculate Foreboding and Occasional Dance Rehearsal?"

Jago laughed, slapping him playfully across the cheek. "You're quite silly, you know? It's charming, and you should use it more. Make your next show an absurdist comedy perhaps?"

"You think I'll have another one?"

"Why wouldn't you? You could put on the worst piece of crap a Madrid stage has ever seen. They still wouldn't drum you out, so long as you're being brave."

Perhaps it was Jago's words or the drink, but he did feel brave. He kissed Jago again, slipping the hand that had been on his chest behind his head, while he reached lower with the other, tracing the faint definition of Jago's stomach until his fingers pushed through a down of soft hairs. Alex's fingers brushed the warm flesh of Jago's cock.

"Sorry," he said, withdrawing.

"I don't recall stopping you. I thought we were being brave?"

Alex inched his way down Jago's body like he was descending a ladder, kissing first his neck, then his chest and nipples. The warm, natural scent of Jago's underarm, dry and clean yet heightened by the summer heat was more than he could resist. He put his nose to it, letting the dark thatch of hair tickle his lips before kissing his way down Jago's flank to his abs. He danced around Jago's midsection, considering his moves as if it were a chessboard. Alex liked to think he knew how to bring a man to several satisfying checks before any 'mating' took place. With Jago, he wanted to get it just right.

He glanced up to see Jago lying on his back, eyes closed, arms resting behind his head, biting his lip as he tried to anticipate Alex's next move. Alex had never kissed muscles so close to the surface surrounding a man's dick before. He enjoyed Jago's grin as he brushed his cheek along the smooth, uncut erection. He stroked the spot beneath Jago's balls with two fingers, pressing just hard enough to elicit a moan and another twitch as he play-bit the inside of Jago's thigh, then caught one of Jago's balls briefly in his mouth before releasing it. He licked away a drop of pre-cum that had smeared his lips, then took the head of Jago's cock in his mouth, expertly working his foreskin back and forth, pushing his tongue into it to savour each drop. The sound of Jago's moan as he abruptly slid his lips down the entire shaft was all the sign he needed to press a little firmer beneath Jago's balls, tweaking the man's nipple with his other hand.

Jago laughed. "You've been holding out on me."

"What's that mean?" Alex asked before resuming service.

"It means you're not so naïve as you let people think."

Taking hold of Alex's shoulders, Jago flipped their positions with surprising dexterity. His erection fell from Alex's mouth, flopping neatly between Alex's legs as he moved to return the favour.

"I'll take that as a complimen—*Oh!*"

"Mmmm," Jago slid his mouth up and down Alex's shaft, suckling his balls and pushing his nose into Alex's pubes as he tongued the hilt. "You should." Within seconds, it was clear Jago enjoyed giving oral pleasure at least as much as he enjoyed receiving. He was coyer about it than Alex, playing patiently with the shaft and balls like each potential movement or drop of pre-cum were a new discovery, a source of fascination he couldn't waste. "You smell good."

"So do you."

"No," Jago glanced down as a gentle chuckle escaped him. "I mean, sometimes the ointment can smell a bit weird the first time you put it on, or even react to the skin. But I think it likes you."

"Your ointment likes me?" Alex laughed. "What do I say to that?"

"I can get you a gag if that will make it easier. Now, shush."

Jago began sucking again, bringing Alex dangerously close to climax before he withdrew. He gently rolled Alex onto his side, flicking his tongue over the crack of Alex's backside.

"Woah, I'm not… I mean, I was not expecting this." A shy expression darkened Alex's face. No discussion had killed more moods mid-flight than this one. "I'm not prepped."

"Understood." Jago kissed Alex gently on the forehead. "Do you enjoy it?"

"Oh gods, yes!"

Jago's kind smile spread into a mischievous grin. "Then trust me. I have my ways."

He rested on his side as Jago continued to play with his body, kiss his neck, and massage between his legs, exploring every opening and crevice for signs of potential pleasure. If Alex wasn't responding, it was for good and simple reason—it was *all* pleasure. Before he could ask Jago if he was sure or protest further, Jago had smeared a little more of the ointment over his erection and was pushing it against Alex's crack. Should he have resisted? Did he trust his body? He trusted Jago well enough, and damn, he did want this.

Accepting the smooth wet length of the shaft as it pushed inside him, Alex grasped Jago's hand tight, kissing it as Jago slid in deeper, pulling Alex's body into his own and kissing his neck. He felt the dark fur of Jago's legs mingled with his, smelled the hint of sweat that could no longer contain itself as their bodies mingled. He tried to turn his head to catch Jago in a kiss, only to gasp as Jago thrilled his prostate with confident thrusts. He whimpered as Jago granted him the kiss he'd desired, moaning into his mouth as they continued fucking in ecstasy. Jago clasped one hand firmly around Alex's shoulders while the other cupped his cock. Alex whimpered as he slid his erection along the warm flesh of Jago's palm, as if they were fucking in unison, Jago pleasuring Alex while Alex hoped this was just the beginning of what they could explore together.

"Don't let go of me," whispered Jago.

Like hell! Alex could have come so easily, but the thought of ending this moment was more than he could bear. Letting go was out of the question. He closed his eyes as the ground beneath them seemed to fall away, Jago's legs wrapped around his, that beautiful, bold cock spearing into him again and again, finding new corners of his insides to pleasure. He could feel their bodies turning in unison, as Jago tightened his grip. "I'm so close," he breathed.

"Just a little more," Jago replied. "I want your first time to last."

Rather than ask what that meant, the decidedly non-virginal Alex pushed his hips back deeper into Jago's. The man eased his grip on Alex's cock without entirely letting go, as their bodies convulsed in unison, locked together, tumbling in what felt like open air. Jago pushed again with such force that Alex opened his eyes. He didn't realise at first that several feet now separated them from the floor, or that the sensation of weightlessness he'd felt while being fucked had been no illusion. In that dim room, surrounded by candles and Jago's collection of occult oddities, their bronzed bodies hovered in place, intertwined like the snakes of the Caduseus. Two Andalusian dogs, floating in each other's lust.

He began to shake. "Jago? Jago what—" The shaking grew more violent, and he began kicking his legs.

"Alex? Alex, close your eyes. Relax. It's all right."

"Jago? What's going on? What the hell?"

"Alex, stop fighting—" The pair of them collapsed to the floor with a sudden bump, falling apart and sprawling across the mat. Jago let out a gasp, rubbing the elbow that had taken the brunt of his fall. "I told you not to fight it."

Alex was still trying to catch his breath, ignoring the pain in the hip he'd landed on. "Fight what? Jago? What was that? What did you do?"

"Perhaps I should have warned or even asked you. But I thought you'd enjoy it much more as a surprise."

"A surprise? One minute you're fucking me and the next, we're floating like Linda Blair in *The Exorcist*."

"While I'm still fucking you, yes."

"*Jago!* That's not the issue. Explain the floating to me."

"If I do, will you promise not to be mad?" Jago held his hands up in front of him, as they got to their feet. "I need you to have an open mind."

"An open…" The absurdity of the scene dawned on Alex before he could finish. There they were, nursing probable bruises after a bout of what had up to that point been the best sex of his young life. It was a scene from some farcical supernatural play, only without wires or effects. "I think it's safe to say my mind is open."

Jago suppressed an obvious smirk as they stood together in all their nakedness. "Can we sit down? What I need to tell you is going to sound a bit strange."

Alex accepted the invitation, waiting patiently for Jago to sit down opposite him, legs folded, composed as he had been when he'd first asked Alex to disrobe. When Jago's answers were not immediately forthcoming, Alex refused to wait any longer. "What was that about, then? It's a neat trick."

"It's not a trick, Alex. Not entirely. It's taken me many years to master the skills. Perhaps I overestimated my own abilities."

"Abilities? You're a magician, then? A conjuring trickster?"

Jago held up a hand to shush him. "Alex, I'm a witch."

CHAPTER SEVEN

Alex's face went blank as he processed what had to be one more gag in this evening of the absurd. "Aren't witches usually women?"

"I assure you, some of us are men. I offer myself as evidence."

"I see. And where's your coven?"

"I've none right now."

"I see. But have you communed with the devil?"

"Notwithstanding the inquisitorial undertones of that question," Jago said, his voice at last wavering with annoyance. "I cannot commune with a being that to the best of my knowledge, does not exist."

"Uhuh. Right. And the tarot?"

"One doesn't need to be a witch to read the tarot."

"I'll bet it doesn't hurt."

"My insights may certainly be sharper, but the methods remain just as I described them to you. Anyone can read tarot in a way that's right for them. Some draw insights from the supernatural. Others from plain old human wisdom."

"And can anyone levitate themselves and their partner mid-coitus as well? Or is that your special trick to whip out at parties?"

"You might have phrased that differently."

Alex took a patient breath, doing his best to understand. "Jago, if I don't start getting some answers that make sense, I swear…"

"You'll what? Run to your friends? The police? I imagine your levitation story would make for a compelling anecdote. Tell them there's a male witch flying up and down the Gran Via looking for the perfect pair of red shoes. I would have had the apartment building propped up on chicken legs, but it's so expensive to do that in Madrid these days."

Alex flinched as Jago took hold of his wrist, but didn't pull away.

"Alex? It is a huge deal for me to reveal this to you. It's only disbelief that keeps people like me safe, even in the twentieth century, at least in Spain. There's a reason I've been living abroad all this time."

"Abroad?" Alex shook his head, every doubt that had occurred to him in the short time he'd known Jago now crowding his brain, demanding to be heard. "That's another thing that doesn't make sense. You look… what? Twenty-four? Twenty-five? *My age*. But you talk about years spent in Mexico and Colombia. You use words like 'abroad.' How old are you, really? You said thirty-eight, but I don't believe you!"

"If I said that magick helps me appear younger than my years, would it release me from having to contrive a number for you? I am old enough to have become the man I am now. That man, Alex, would like very much to help you, if you'll let me."

"Help me how?"

"I'm still an admirer of the arts. I have an eye. I have money. I have the trust of your Joanna too, I think."

"The trust of *my* Joanna?" Alex blinked several times, but Jago's expression remained earnest. "You will *not* tell Joanna or Vicente what you just told me."

"What else must I do to win your confidence? To convince you of how rare it is for someone to earn mine? I understand if my nature frightens you. I'll understand if you choose to leave. I've cast no love spells on you, nor made you drink any potions. You're not a prisoner, Alex. I want us to be clear on this. As for the levitation…" Jago shrugged, guilt at last seeping into his face. "I wanted you to experience something extraordinary, and it blew up in my face. I'm sorry."

In a more playful mood, Alex might have pointed out that nothing had blown up for either of them, but the moment had passed. "And what about the pigeon? The taxidermy story? You *did* bring a dead pigeon inside."

"I did," Jago admitted, standing and walking over to a large oak closet. He propped open both doors, revealing four shelves stocked with bottles, pots and jars of every shape and size. He carefully placed the ointment he'd used to massage Alex on the lowest shelf, and stepped aside, letting Alex get a good look at the pantry of horrors that included a jar full of bird's claws and what looked to be a pickled frog surrounded by seaweed. Alex checked out once he spied the jar full of tiny eyeballs. "I'm not above shopping for supplies, but many of the necessary ingredients must be sourced first-hand. I'm happy to describe them for you, though I see by the look on your face that we are not going to share this interest. At least, not yet."

"I…" Alex began, still trying not to gag. "Disinterested is not the word I'd use."

"Horrified, then? I can accept that."

"Oh, come on, man. You've got to admit this is a lot to drop on someone."

"For both of us." Jago closed the cupboard and locked it. "I said that to you the moment I knew we would be having this conversation. I learned very early what my gifts made me, especially in Andalusia."

"A *brujo*?"

"In plainest, most reductive terms. In Mexico, that word has other, more positive connotations. You must go. A beautiful culture, Mexico. Catholic faithful? Yes, but they celebrate death for what it brings to life. The *brujo* and the *bruja* are revered for the wisdom they bring to a community. Not that I was open about things, you understand, but I'd at least no fear of growing my talents. Before that? In Colombia, magick is accepted as a silent yet active part of everyday life. It offered me the perfect place to observe how it worked until I was ready to embrace it myself. Such ways we've lost here. A great nation with one of the richest histories on Earth, lasting hundreds and hundreds of years. Visigoths, Moors… and what are we known for? The genocide of the New World, a murderous Inquisition, and a miserable dictator who murdered poets to make his point."

"So why don't you go back?"

A sly smile made Alex wonder if Jago was about to make some flippant remark, but none came. "The most valuable thing I've learned in Colombia, Mexico, Spain, or the realms we traverse beyond—"

"The what, now?"

"Let's come back to that. The most important thing is to follow the power. When you feel something—a force, a person, a place—drawing you, to resist is to invite disaster. Or, at least, to invite stagnation, which is its own disaster for a curious mind."

"If you plan on making me your student, I'm not interested."

Jago's boisterous laugh filled the tiny room as he put his clothes back on. "If it were only so simple, I might have taken a companion long ago. No, Alex, you're not my acolyte. I desire nothing more than to see those who catch lightning in a bottle fulfil their potential. It empowers me."

"Empowers?" Alex asked, reaching for his own pile of clothes. "You mean it fuels your magic?"

"Again, reductive, but astute. I nourish them as they nourish me. You're familiar with the rule of three, of course?"

Alex's elementary witchcraft was rustier than his French.

"Whatever you put out into the universe, returns to you threefold. A wise caution against casting spells of destruction, anger, manipulation, or vengeance. I grow my powers through creation, Alex, just like yours. It is merely a different kind."

Fully dressed, Jago swung open the door that had admitted them to his sacred space. His chamber of potions, spells, meditation, conjuring, incantation and… who knew what else. "I'd invite you upstairs, but there is somewhere else I need to take you."

"Somewhere else? Jago, I'm very tired. It's almost…" He trailed off, realising he'd no idea what time it was.

"Early enough. Please?"

Alex flipped through all the possibilities in his mind. Jago silently let him, until he reached the door, unable to ignore one final question. "Lorca?"

"What of him?"

"You speak as if you knew the man. Dali and Buñuel, too, for that matter."

"I know the poet better than anyone. But I think you've a story far more your own to tell than *Blood Wedding*, yes?"

As Alex put on his shoes, he found himself unable to dispute either statement.

*　　*　　*

Perhaps it was the effects of the massage, the levitation, learning Jago's true vocation, his tiredness, or the sudden abundance of streetlights that had disoriented him, but Alex had no idea where he was. Not one street into which they turned seemed familiar, and by the time—ten minutes, twenty, or an hour, Alex couldn't say— they reached their destination, a dark entryway lit only by a small, glowing red sign that read *La Otra Cava*, he was no longer certain how to get home.

"Jago?"

Instead of answering, Jago knocked four times on a door made of the shiniest black wood Alex had ever seen. When no response came, he knocked again, four sharp raps, then one with such force, Alex half expected him to break a hole in the door. A panel slid noisily aside. From behind it, came steady, heavy breath, thick with wheezing, as if every breath was pure labour.

"***Karpvus vak, tel Vach?***" the voice rasped without further explanation.

"***Vien. Toch. Vach matg. Krrrrr.***"

The breathing continued, a solitary sound in the otherwise still night. It unnerved Alex, to whom Madrid and silence seemed the most unnatural bedfellows. A loud clang startled him before the door slid aside, revealing not a speaker, but a long corridor as dark as the door. A dim red light marked the corner around which they should turn. There was no sign of the gravel-voiced speaker anywhere.

"What was that language?" Alex asked, curiosity holding back anxiety as he peered down the hall.

Jago squeezed his hand. "I honestly don't know."

Emboldened when Jago didn't let go, Alex allowed him to take them across the threshold together. For some reason, he'd expected their shoes to clip loudly on the dark wooden floor, but he could barely hear them at all. What he could hear instead now, was music. Soft music beholden to no discernible rules but its own, like jazz or some Eastern genre he didn't understand. Of course, people said the same thing about flamenco, and probably about whatever Alaska and her band were doing. In another setting, it might have repelled him, made him question his choice to be here so late at night with a man he barely knew. A witch he barely knew. 'I honestly don't know.' The confession comforted him more than it probably should.

They emerged in a tiny theatre, which for reasons he couldn't explain, had been exactly what Alex had expected. As they took their seats in the second last row, Alex stared agog the disaster strewn across the stage. It was as if the theatre itself had flooded. Sections of boards floated an inch above the black water surface, islands of normality nonetheless ripped apart. Boxes added dimension to the milieu. Scraps of burlap sack hung from the ceiling like the boughs of swamp-dwelling trees. In lieu of a curtain, another creek of dark water separated the audience from the grim diorama.

They weren't alone in the theatre. He saw the back of an old woman's head with hair tied in a grey bun. Two younger men sat a few rows down, and near the front, a couple with a small child at their side. What family brought a child of nine or ten to the theatre in the wee hours of the morning?

"How do you know this place? What is it?"

When Jago showed no sign of having heard him, he let his other questions go. Why was the theatre full of water? Was it a flooding accident, or an extremely sophisticated set? Why was a show starting so late? Why had nobody asked them for admission or tickets? What had become of the man who'd granted them entry in such cryptic tongue? One futile question followed the next. Jago's only answer was to place a solitary hand on Alex's thigh.

The house lights dimmed.

"Ladies and gentlemen," purred a distinguished voice in English. *"We welcome, for your consideration and delectation, Jacqueline."*

Alex had already placed a hand over Jago's. It tightened as a barefoot woman in a flowing white dress followed the dry patches to centre stage. The long black hair that hung in front of her eyes made her look like a ghost from a Japanese horror film. Admittedly, Alex had only seen two, but that image had stayed with him, just as it had clearly influenced the director of whatever opus had just begun.

A song accompanied the woman's steps, the indiscernible words mere additions to the effect being created as she kneeled at the water, reached her fingers into it and dragged them across, sending a ripple that seemed to heighten the music throughout the theatre. Alex shivered. She did it again, with smooth, gentle confidence. There was no aggression, not that it was easy to see any emotion as her hair continued to obscure her face. The song's beautiful gibberish grew lounder as she began reaching deeper into the water. It dampened the sleeves of her dress, but didn't deter her as she reached deeper, deeper still, allowing the waters to reach almost to her shoulders. She dipped her hair in them, soaking her tresses before whipping hem around like a weapon, sprinkling the set and the sparse crowd. Alex stole a glance at Jago's expression. It was anxious, almost fearful, even as he bit his lip, obviously enthralled.

For the briefest second, Alex thought he could make out the woman's face, but it was gone behind a curtain of damp hair before he could be sure. Then, the entire head was gone, dunked beneath the waters with a loud, solid *ke-plonk*.

They tensed their mutual grip with anticipation, waiting for her to surface. The water must have been deep for the actor to submerge her head entirely. How long could she hold her breath? The music had taken on a dull, stifled quality, its rhythm breaking with irregular syncopation, as if it too, were struggling to breathe underwater. Seconds later, she began beating her hands and feet against the stage as if trying to push herself free.

"Jago?" Alex's voice was barely a whisper. He doubted Jago had heard it at all.

They both jumped in their seats as she pulled her head abruptly from the water, dragging with it the shape of a man who'd pressed his fingers around her neck. Beyond his damp blonde hair and broad, athletic shoulders, Alex could at last make out the woman's face.

"Joanna!" he cried out.

Jago clapped his hand over Alex's mouth. He watched helplessly as the actors struggled, and Joanna rolled over on her back, only to be pulled towards the water again.

"Stop!" Jago hissed in his ear. "You must stop!"

Joanna struggled against the grip of the blond man, who'd slipped beneath the waters once more with only a firm hand gripping Joanna's hair and another on her throat to announce his presence. Alex pushed Jago away just as Joanna broke free of the assault, retreating upstage and assuming a defensive posture on her haunches, hands outstretched like claws, keeping the man at bay. He slid smoothly from the waters, his naked body flopping at her side like a seal. She repositioned herself to give him space, but on dry land, some unseen force had sapped him of all energy. He dragged himself along the stage, willing each arm to pull and each foot to push him along like some ancient fish learning to use evolution's first feeble attempt at limbs. When he at last flopped over on his back, his face was filled with pain. It was another face Alex knew. A body he'd held. A dick he'd sucked.

"Vicente," he whispered. "Jago, we have to—"

"Alex, I beg you." Jago grasped his hand again.

His mind raced, not knowing what to believe. In no universe would sweet Vicente ever do intentional harm to Joanna, or anyone, for that matter. He also wasn't an actor, which meant that the awful rasping sounds now coming from his throat had to be real.

"We have to help him." Alex didn't know why he was still whispering. What was wrong with the rest of them? Not a gasp. Not a cry. Not one voice had been raised in compassion or concern. No reaction at all. He winced as Jago pressed hard into a tender spot on his wrist, silently shaking his head. On stage, he saw Joanna hovering over Vicente's body as it gasped for breath. She gently rolled him to the water's edge, where she dipped her hair, squeezing the liquid over Vicente's body as if bathing unseen wounds. The movement seemed to steady his breath as she washed his chest, stomach, legs and exposed cock with her hair, dipping it in the water as she needed. When she was done, she rested one hand at the centre of his chest, the other between his legs.

"*Doch mat. Kahven leth?*"

Vicente's lips were moving, but the voice was the one that had admitted them to the club.

"*Gel-VASHtuq sverehistei.* *How does it taste now?*"

That last part had been in English, which Vis also didn't speak.

Joanna lowered her mouth to Vicente's chest, dotting it with kisses that slowly made their way from its centre to one of his nipples. She bit him so hard, blood flowed. Vicente screamed. Alex was up from his seat and running toward the stage before Jago could stop him. A glimpse of the old woman sitting two rows down from them startled him so hard, he tripped down the stairs. Staring at him from her seat was a skeletal, rictus grin of approval, matched in death on the faces of the couple further down, and in the parents with their child. Six souls, long dead, skin shrunken to bones, organs long melted.

"Alex," Vicente sobbed, reaching out to him. "Alex!"

"I'm coming, Vis!"

"Alex, you mustn't!" Jago's plea fell on deaf ears as Alex used a chair to pull himself to his feet.

"Joanna, what are you do—" He stumbled forward to the stage and plunged headlong into the water, going in over his head before he had time to draw breath. He dispelled his disbelief long enough to kick off his shoes and try to tread the strangely warm waters. Alex tumbled over and over in the dark, until he'd lost any sense of buoyancy, neither sinking, nor floating. He had to get to the surface. For Vis. For himself. Could he stand up? The waters couldn't possibly be so deep that—

The sensation of hard stone on his bare feet jarred him. Standing up, he burst from the water, which now reached only to his knees. He flailed like a madman in the dry night air, mopping water from his face and eyes, looking down at his soaked clothes. He was standing knee-deep in the waters of the fountain, with the bronze image of the fallen Lucifer towering over him, a hive of daemonic faces laughing in unison. Otherwise, he was alone.

Dawn's first rays reflected a glint of gold in the water. It was the ping pong ball Jago had tossed away earlier. Alex watched it abruptly sink to the bottom, releasing a small bubble as it went.

CHAPTER EIGHT

"You look exhausted, lovely." Without being asked, Victoria ducked behind the counter and poured him an enormous cup of black coffee. "I know you kids like your partying, but I need you sharp, understood?"

"I'm sorry." He accepted the cup with rueful gratitude. "I'm okay, really."

It wasn't as if walking home had clarified things for him. The emerging dawn light had brought with it only more questions. He'd called Vicente and Joanna from the first payphone he'd found. A sleepy and annoyed Vis had informed him both of them had not only gotten home safely some hours prior but had been fast asleep. He'd mumbled an apology, and lacking a plausible explanation for his panic, had hung up.

That assurance that Vis and Joanna were in one piece had been the only thing keeping him from marching back to Jago's apartment and demanding answers. That is, the only thing besides the fact that his questions made no bloody sense. Had any of it been real? If not, he couldn't even be mad at Jago.

"What did you take?" Victoria asked as he sipped.

"Huh? Nothing?"

"I know the look, dear. No bother, just asking as a mother with a son not much younger than you. I have no idea what they're passing around these days, and do you think he'll tell me anything?"

Alex knew a lie was the clearest way out of this. "Just a joint. There might have been some coke."

"Might have been?"

"I don't know. I can't afford that stuff."

"For the record, that's *not* how you should ask me for a raise."

The door to the café swung open, admitting a handful of young people whose brightly coloured clothes clashed with their sombre dispositions. For a moment, Alex thought he recognised them.

"Good morning," Victoria called, offering them a smile before tilting her head to signal Alex's cue. She opened new a bag of potatoes and started peeling.

Alex hastily put down his coffee, straightened his shirt, and went over. "What can I get you?"

The heads of the two closest to him lolled on their necks like macabre dolls, considering his request like he'd delivered it in Beat poetry. "Orange juice. Fresh," the man said at last.

"Tostada," said the other bobble head, a woman whose electric blue lipstick both repelled and fascinated Alex. He passed no comment on the unlit cigarette between her fingers.

"Tortilla, please," said the bright young woman in the pink and black dress, sitting opposite the man in the red jacket, whose frizzy shock of dark hair and round, appealing face seemed the most familiar. He was gazing out the window, lost in thought.

"Sir?"

Red Jacket turned with a distracted smile. "Coffee, thank you."

Alex returned to the counter with their orders, cutting a slice of tortilla and preparing the drinks. As he poured the coffee, he remembered where he'd seen the man who'd ordered it; the *Pepi Luci Bom* screening, though Alex couldn't remember his name.

"What was he even doing up there?" asked Blue Lipstick of her friends.

"I don't know. Peach is devastated."

"Who's Peach?"

"The latest. Anyway, have they fished him out yet?"

"Of course they have. Think they're going to bloody leave him there for tourists to see?"

"Both of you, stop it."

Alex hadn't meant to eavesdrop. But how many Peaches could there be in Madrid? Only Red Jacket, who'd ordered the coffee remained silent as he approached.

"Thanks."

Alex couldn't tell which one had thanked him, but he decided to be bold. "What was that about Peach?"

The Beat poetry stare returned. "What?" asked Blue Lipstick.

"Peach? We met at a show recently if it's the person I'm thinking of. Is she okay?"

The more cheerful woman sitting opposite Red Jacket rescued him. "Not really. If you met her at a show, you must know Si-Man."

"Yes?" Alex sensed this was not the time to weigh in as a theatre critic.

"He drowned last night. A man walking his dog found him floating in the pools around Templo de Debod."

It took all the concentration Alex had to keep his hands from shaking as he gripped the tray containing their orders.

"I'm surprised you haven't heard, being friends with Peach and all." The one who'd ordered the orange juice cocked his head at it, flicking his dangling earring back like it annoyed him.

Alex hurriedly put the juice down, then the frittata before reaching for the coffee. The suddenly lighter tray began to wobble in his hand, spilling dribbles of coffee over the cup's edge.

Red Jacket took it from the tray before he could spill any more. "Thanks."

Alex nodded, embarrassed. "Sorry. I can get you another—"

"It's fine." He went back to staring out the window.

He took a moment to steady his nerves. Blue Lipstick lifted the plate of tomato-smeared toast from the tray with an irritated scoff.

Alex mouthed a silent apology, lowering the tray. "I really liked your movie."

Red Jacket said nothing at first, then a quiet "thanks" as he continued to stare out the window. The others turned to Alex with expressions that landed somewhere between bemusement, disdain and pity. Forcing a smile, Alex withdrew to the counter, his gut tight from his failed attempt to end the exchange on a high note. Victoria was nowhere to be seen. When he lifted his head again, he saw Jago's tanned, nervous face looking back at him across the counter. They stared at one another in silence, ignoring the street outside and the mumbled conversation at the director's table.

"Coffee?" Alex finally asked with the detachment he'd grant any customer at the end of an exhausting day. It was barely noon.

"Will you join me?"

"I'm working."

"Alex, please?"

"No. Jago, please just order something or leave. I'm not doing this."

"Doing what? Can't we even discuss last night?"

"I wouldn't know how to start."

"Then let me." They looked up as the door at the back of the kitchen swung open and Victoria returned from her cigarette break. "But not here."

"And not now. You seriously have to bother me at work?"

"Last time, you thought it was sweet. Besides, this is not the work you're serious about."

Alex caught a glance from Victoria as she unwrapped a tray of pig's ears, a dish he'd never developed a taste for. "I'm serious enough to not want to get fired."

"You're making excuses. You know she won't fire you, just as you know I'm the only person who'll believe what you saw last night. The only person who can assure you you're not crazy."

Alex brushed the warm wooden counter with his fingers, hoping another customer would pull him away. But none came, and the one busy table's occupants were lost in their own private conversation. "I didn't see anything because none of it was real."

"Bullshit. We both know what we saw."

"Fine. Drinking with Vis and Joanna in the park? Going back to your apartment? Yes, all of that happened. Then I left. I don't know what you gave me to drink, but—"

"You're saying I *drugged* you?" Jago began to ball his fists, shoulders near quivering. "I'm sorry, Alex, but if you must lie to yourself, I'll not go along with it."

"You can believe what you like. Just leave me alone." He gathered up a half-dozen menus that didn't need refreshing, straightening, or cleaning and stalked off to the end of the counter.

Jago followed. "Is Joanna okay?"

Alex turned an indignant glare on him. "Yes. So is Vicente, or did you forget about what happened to him?"

"Then you know what we saw to be true as well as I do. I'm pleased to hear they're both—"

"Stop it, will you? Whatever *we* saw, they didn't experience any of it. I called them this morning. Vicente was pissed off, but he's fine, and so is Joanna. As for… *what* you are…"

Jago tilted his head patiently. "Go on."

"I don't care. That's your business. Religious freedom, blah, blah. I appreciate what you've done for us, Jago but I can't do this. I can't."

"I've not asked you to do anything. Simply accompany me last night, which you did."

"So? There's nothing more to discuss. Now order something or leave."

"Coffee, please. Now, what I'm trying to tell you—"

"Coffee does not come with my conversation in this establishment."

"Damn it, Alex. How often do you think I share an experience like that with someone else, even a man I fancy?"

Alex looked up in time to see the snootier two of the director's friends avert their eyes.

"I can make them leave," Jago said.

"You'll do no such thing. Just keep your voice down, or better yet—"

"If you want me to leave you alone so badly, then of course I shall. But at least do yourself and your show the courtesy of asking your star and stage manager."

"Vicente's not fond of you."

"So I've observed. I don't need his fondness, just his trust."

"You *definitely* don't have that, nor mine."

"No?" Jago folded his arms. "Vicente, I understand, but from you? That does wound me. You've been, forgive me, a bloody prick ever since I came in here and over what? An admittedly provocative show I didn't create that's made me as curious as you are?"

"You kept telling me not to interfere. Why? Damn it, my friends were being hurt."

"You said your friends were safely in bed until you woke them in the wee hours with an unnecessary phone call. Yet they were also there, on stage. We know this because I saw the same show you did." He leaned closer, whispering to Alex over the counter. "Only makes it more intriguing, no?"

"Look after things while I'm gone, won't you Alex?" said Victoria, hanging up her apron and gathering her purse. "Matteo was short this morning, but he promised he'd be restocked by noon."

"Of course," Alex replied, trying to ignore Jago, even though Victoria refused to do the same.

She leaned close to his ear. "And your boyfriend popping in isn't going to be a daily habit, is it?"

Alex offered her a sheepish smile, which Victoria, already halfway to the front door, ignored. He turned back to Jago. "Why did you try and stop me? Don't tell me it was out of courtesy to the other patrons. They were *dead*." He'd meant to whisper, but the looks he now got from the occupied table spoke to how miserably he'd failed. The customers began to gather their things. Nice going, idiot. "I'll get you that coffee."

From the corner of his eye, he watched Red Jacket approach the counter with a fistful of pesetas. He also saw Jago watching the man with keen interest.

Putting the money on the counter, Red Jacket offered Alex a shy smile. "Thanks again for coming to the movie."

"Thank you," Alex replied, trying to fix his professional demeanour back in place.

Jago finally spoke. "The next one will be better."

"Pardon?" Red Jacket frowned.

"I thought you liked it?" offered Alex, not sure what else to say.

"I did," Jago said. "I also know the next one will be better."

Visibly perplexed, Red Jacket gave each of them a nod before joining his friends outside.

Alex set the coffee down in front of Jago.

"You seem rattled," Jago said.

"Why aren't you? You've seen it all before, I suppose? Well, abracadabra and yippee fuck for you."

"I don't mean rattled by the show. Something else has happened. I felt it from your customers as well. A death, perhaps?"

Alex swallowed. Was Jago an empath now? A psychic? Besides, 'rattled' wasn't the right word. He hadn't felt much of anything about Si-Man's death, or what it meant for them.

"He's dead."

"Who?"

"The performance artist we saw last night. He drowned. Just… it seems weird, is all."

"Oh, that's tragic. So… what does that mean for your show?"

Alex's eyes widened twice, first at the insensitivity, then again as the implication hit home. "I haven't thought about that. This really isn't the time."

"Bull's balls it isn't! Look, the poor bloke's dead. Let others mourn him. We, my friend, have a show to rehearse and less time than ever to make it shine."

"You aren't serious? And what do you mean *we*?"

"Alex," Jago took both his hands and clasped them tight. "I commend you not wanting to be the arsehole here, so I'll do it for you. Nobody comes out to see independent theatre produced by—forgive me—some nobody from the provinces in February. You would have been playing to an empty theatre and Joanna's extraordinary talents would be all for nought."

"Look, even *if* Maria changes her mind, she's right about one thing. We don't have any sales. We can't turn that around in—"

"Let me worry about Maria and your sales. We'll paper the damn place for opening night if we have to. You're a solid talent, Alex, but Joanna? Joanna *must* be seen."

Alex heard the chimes of the front door go, but instead of Victoria, the woman of the hour strode in, prompting his jaw to drop. "Joanna? You're… you're here?"

"Yes?" She removed a large red sun hat and beamed at them.

"You never come to see me here, and where's Vicente?"

"Vicente, darling, is sleeping off a late night and a rude awakening. It's lucky for you, I'm a deep sleeper."

"About that? It's not like you to be around in daylight."

"Careful. A lady could take offence at that remark. Fortunately, I'm nobody's lady. Jago!" She took him in a warm hug and kissed both his cheeks. "Thank you again for saving us last night. It would have been a wretched bore without you."

Ahem, thought Alex. Now who had reason to take offence?

"Thank you for sharing what you've created with us. I know you said it needs work, and I'll let you and Alex be the judge of that, but from where I sat?" Jago kissed his fingertips before splaying them like a chef in rapture. "Meanwhile, Alex has some good news."

Alex's eyes widened again.

"Good for us, at least. Tell her."

"I… He's dead."

"What?"

"Si-Man's dead. They found him in the pond around Templo de Debod last night."

Joanna stared at him, eyes as wide as Alex's had been moments before. Then, she punched him in the arm. "Don't scare me like that. I thought you meant someone we knew or cared about."

"Joanna!"

"And how does one drown in the pond around the Templo de Debod? It might be the most unique and extraordinary talent he ever demonstrated. So, what then? We're…" She gripped his shoulders, the annoyance on her face giving way to excitement. "Does Maria know? Are we back on?"

"Okay, I give you both props for artistic commitment, but a man is dead"

"And there's not a damn thing we can do about that, Alex," Jago reminded him. "If you want to honour his memory, put on a show people like him will want to emulate for years. Hell, dedicate your opening night to him if that makes you feel better, but do it. Joanna's ready."

"I am, and so is Vis. Alex, this is fate. Horrible, cruel fate perhaps, but for us? We're doing this."

"Actually, dedicating the opening night to him will probably help fill seats," Jago said, stroking his throat, thoughtfully. "Though I don't suppose you had any friends in common who could help get the word out?"

"Okay, fine. Fine. Just… let me talk to Maria."

"We can go talk to her now." Joanna replaced her hat, beaming at Jago as he eased his weight off the counter. "Don't worry, darling. We'll take care of everything."

"There's no *we*, Joanna. Not with him." The pair's hurt expressions almost made him feel guilty. "It's not personal, Jago, but this is our project. I'll comp you to opening night, but—"

"Oh, you'll comp me, will you? Lovely." Jago rolled his eyes. "Sorry, that was flippant, but really, Alex?"

"It's just that after last night…" he trailed off, not sure where to begin. He could hardly recount the details of the show they'd seen to Joanna. Hell, even with Jago, he hadn't gotten to the bit about finding himself alone in the waters of the Morningstar fountain, and he'd no idea how to explain that little act of teleportation, even to a witch. On that note, Joanna didn't need to know Jago was a witch, did she?

"Last night?" she asked, her eyebrows raised. "You two screwed, didn't you? I knew it."

"No. I mean, yes, but that's not…"

"No? Yes? Which is it?"

"Joanna!"

"Jago?"

Jago shook his head. "Careful, Alex. You're drowning a lot faster than Si-Man right now."

"Okay, *that* was not called for."

"Alex!" Joanna barked, shutting them both up as she took Alex's hand and turned to Jago. "Will you please give us a moment?"

Jago took his now surely cold coffee to a table near the far wall.

"I don't care what you two got up to or what drama it's now caused," Joanna hissed once he was out of earshot. "All I know is that man brings out something in me that I need, something greater than anything I've ever felt on stage in my life."

Alex gave a cold nod. "Then perhaps he should direct you?"

"Hey, none of that." She gave his hand a firm squeeze. "This is your vision, your show, your direction. I know Jago buttered me up last night, but you were there. You saw how much work it still needs. That means I need both of you, and I need Vis. You as my director, Vis as stage manager and Jago just… *there*. Alex, try to understand. Please?"

Alex recognised the mania that had crept into her eye. He'd seen it in dozens of acquaintances, whose minds and passions had begun to work overtime with the precious energy of an idea they could all but see—or in this case, a muse they couldn't let go. "You don't fancy him, do you?"

"Bitch, I will hit you again. Besides, when have Vicente or I ever muscled in on one of your paramours? And as Pam Grier might say, 'damn, he fine!'"

That made Alex laugh, which triggered a warm smile from Jago. As their eyes met, however, every anxiety and doubt returned to him. Jago was a witch. Not some charlatan messing around with tarot cards and props or claiming to commune with the dark ones. They'd floated above the floor while having sex. Then had come the awful play, where he'd watched his dearest friends commit acts of terrible violence. Then Si-Man's death. He didn't know where to begin explaining any of it to Joanna.

"He…" Alex paused, not wanting to seem foolish or paranoid, nor dismissive of his own doubts. "Would you believe it if I said he frightens me?"

"You?" She laughed. "Perhaps you're more nervous than I realised. Admittedly, when we saw *Alien*, I was too busy comforting Vis to give your nerves a thought."

"I'm serious, Joanna. You don't find him weird? Eccentric?"

She lowered her head, though her eyes remained full with mischief. "Find me one person worth our time who's not."

The door swung open, admitting Victoria and ending their conversation.

Joanna withdrew with a smile as Jago joined her, blowing Alex a kiss as he went. "We'll take care of Maria, darling. You just keep being brilliant."

Alex watched them go, absentmindedly scooping up the money Red Jacket had left on the counter and putting it in the register.

Victoria dropped a packet of fresh sausage in front of him. "Keep being brilliant, won't you, with that slicer?"

He rolled his eyes, unable to resist a smile.

CHAPTER NINE

"I'd feel better if we had a run before showing Maria."

"I know that." Vicente's voice was a font of patience. "I'm with you, only Maria's not going to wait around until seven. We do this now, or we lose the space again."

"Seriously?" Alex asked. "The guy only died last night. She can't have replacements lined up already, surely?"

"All I know, is if we want to be at the front of that queue, Joanna's got to knock Maria flat on her vermouth-soaked arse."

"And us too, apparently."

"I've seen it. Well, bits of it. What she's been willing to show me, anyway. I don't know, man. She was up before I was this morning. You said she came to the café?"

"She did."

"Wild."

"Why so?"

"Come on, Alex. You know she hates going out before dark."

Alex frowned. While Joanna's nocturnal habits were no secret, it still felt strange to have them confirmed by her boyfriend, partner, and, presumably, closest confidante. "You're saying you've never seen her go out during the day?"

"I did not say that. I'm saying she hates it, and when she does go out before sundown, she usually dresses like a penitent during Holy Week. This morning? She couldn't have been merrier."

Alex could hardly deny the truth of this. Admittedly, Joanna would have made a very fetching nun, though an odd one in terms of behaviour. "Where's Jago?"

"Your new assistant is with the talent, talking over her latest changes."

Alex took a moment to breathe. "The hell he is. They said they were going to talk to Maria."

"That they did, and Maria put them on the spot. Deliver a killer audition for her *tonight* or fuck off until February. So, here we are. I thought you'd be pleased."

"Pleased?"

Vicente raised a sarcastic smile with little enthusiasm.

"Oh, come on, Vis. I mean yes, I'm attracted to him, but…" The list of strange coincidences and nightmarish visions returned to Alex's mind. He could no more recite them to Vicente than he could to Joanna. "Aren't you?"

"What?"

"Attracted to him?"

"He's not my type. Good taste in wine, though."

"I haven't forgiven you for that."

"You haven't forgiven *me*? You left me waiting like an idiot for more than an hour, and don't get me started on that call this morning. Why were you even awake?"

Alex covered his face with his hands. "I know, I'm sorry. This isn't..." He put his arms around Vicente and hugged him tight. "I'm sorry."

It took only a second's hesitation for Vicente to return the gesture. "You know, the only reason I haven't bounced this guy into the street is what he's bringing out in Joanna. I've never seen her like this before. She's in love."

Breaking from their hug, Alex raised an eyebrow.

"Not with him. I mean with herself and the dance. It's been two days, man." Vicente shrugged, scratching the back of his neck while pushing his other hand deeper into his pocket. "I can't explain it. He's doing something right."

Alex gave a slow nod, weighing how much of the truth Vicente deserved against how much would confuse and terrify him. Hell, how much of it could Alex believe himself? "I think I might know what, but I'll have to tell you later, and you can't tell anyone. *No one*, Vis."

"Okay, way to freak me out right before rehearsal." Vicente shook his head. "Sorry, I just... had the weirdest dream last night."

Alex's throat tightened. "Go on."

"Like I was a fish or something, but stuck on dry land. I don't even know how I got there. I felt my body bleeding like hooks had gone through it. I couldn't breathe. I don't even remember it ending, certainly not when I woke up. It just stopped. I guess I kept sleeping. Isn't that crazy?"

"Did you tell Joanna?"

Vicente shook his head, scratching his forearm. "And harsh her buzz? It's probably just nicotine withdrawal, anyway."

"Withdrawal? You're trying to quit again, mid-rehearsals?"

"I'm your stage manager." Vicente gave him a friendly slap on the shoulder. "Don't talk to me about masochism."

"Oh hardy-ha-ha. Vis, you know I support you in everything, but right now, *have one*. I don't need you agitated out of your mind while we're trying to win Maria over. Speaking of… Shit! Lighting cues?"

Vicente shrugged, looking at the stage and shaking his head. "Joanna said to wing it."

"To what?"

"To make it up as I go."

"I know what it means, Vis. She's not the director."

"I know that, but what choice do I have? She's reworked the choreography from scratch. Even *if* we had a run through before Maria arrived, you wouldn't have time to work anything out between us. You make your notes and I'll take them. In the meantime, try to look confident, like it was your idea."

Alex pinched the bridge of his nose.

"Listen, I know it feels like they're going over your head, but I've been here all afternoon, Alex. They keep talking about your vision, wanting to make this something that's just you. Let's just use this run-through to get Maria onboard. We'll get our show back, then, you and Joanna change whatever you like, and I'll make it look pretty. Sound good?"

Alex stared at the dim lights hitting the black surface of the stage, letting the silence of the theatre wrap itself around him. "It just feels weird."

"How the guy died, you mean?"

"All of it, Vis. You don't think…" He trailed off, again unsure what to say.

Vicente rescued him with another hug. "I've got you, man. You know I've always got you."

Not 'we,' but 'I.' The distinction wasn't lost on Alex. "Go smoke. I need you back in the box and sharp."

Vicente grinned, reaching for his back pocket as he withdrew. "Last one today. You'll hold me to that, mister director."

Alex resisted the urge to bum a cigarette for himself.

*　　*　　*

On an 'oh shit' list that had seemed to grow longer with each passing minute, Alex had barely thought about where to sit for their command performance. Sitting behind Maria might make her uncomfortable, even if he by some miracle managed to resist scanning her body language for any sign of a response. Sitting alongside her, trying to steal glimpses of her face would be worse, while sitting anywhere in front, with her eyes boring into the back of his head seemed no less awful. He'd finally settled for the back far-left corner, as close to the tech booth as possible.

Maria had been polite and kind, of course, but her tired demeanour and barely contained impatience said plenty about her expectations, and the fact that neither Joanna nor Jago had come out to greet her had only frayed Alex and Vicente's nerves further. Vicente began to dim the lights, pausing as Jago finally came onstage, dressed neat as an usher in top to toe black. He offered Maria a slight bow and a smile, then took his seat next to Alex.

"Hell of a time for you to show your face," Alex said.

"How about you trust Joanna?" Jago squeezed his hand. "And perhaps, trust yourself to let *Blood Wedding* go?"

This hadn't been a command, but a request, as if Alex's answer mattered to him. This, in Alex's short experience of Jago, seemed strange, and request or no, it wasn't like he had a choice. He allowed Jago to squeeze his hand tight, drawing a strange reassurance from it as Vicente lowered the house lights.

Harsh string notes jarred Alex's nerves. He didn't know where Joanna and Jago had managed to find an entirely new score at such short notice, though it wouldn't have surprised him to learn they'd workshopped it in a hash-soaked fugue that afternoon. He closed his eyes and tried to relax. Jago slid his hand across Alex's, stroking it before taking hold again. Alex neither liked or disliked the music, but its discordant quality penetrated his body like a vine finding cracks in a decaying wall, wrapping itself around the questions that had spent the day dancing through his mind.

Blood Wedding couldn't have been further from it.

He closed his eyes, remembering Joanna and Vicente on that watery stage, the grim pantomime they'd played and the dead faces of the audience members. He focused on Jago's hand and allowed his discomfort to pass, remembering instead the strange beauty Jago had seen and tried to show him. Much like their strange floating tryst, he'd not been ready. How could one be ready? He'd been on trips before, ingesting whatever substances were on offer in search of that special something *different*. Jago was certainly that, but the sensation that filled him now was well beyond it.

When he opened his eyes again, Joanna was on stage, turning her head, stroking the back of her fingers along her neck. Black-painted nails stood out against her skin, and Alex jumped when for a fleeting instant she appeared to puncture her neck with them. The graceful extension of her arms guided delicate yet confident steps, like she was mapping the stage, moving from platform to platform, like a newborn exploring a world alien to her.

Possessed with sudden assurance, Joanna's movements became bolder and swifter, each movement and breath an unspoken word, the music mere background noise. Alex felt his heart beat an irregular rhythm and his breath moved with irregular syncopation, in time with each of Joanna's movements.

He felt Jago squeeze his hand once more before all breath left his body, and darkness erased the stage. A single spotlight returned, revealing Joanna on her knees, looking up as if she'd just spied God. Alex imagined her leaning back toward her heels, chest arching to the ceiling, offering herself up to the spirit that had possessed her dance. And so, she did.

He imagined her sliding her hand along the stage before her body rolled after it. She curled into a ball before abruptly lifting her head, just to see if God was still watching. Yet Joanna was in conversation with something much greater. They both were.

His mind conjured myths of the garden and the tree of knowledge that had unleashed the deadly sin of curiosity, and so Joanna reached for the fruit. He considered the cruelty of a god imagined to disguise the viciousness and solidify the control of the men who'd invented him. He jumped as Joanna screamed the scream of every woman to have lost her own spirit or essence to such men. Together, they summoned the scream of every mother to have lost a child in the name of power, greed, ego, or religion.

Joanna's tears flowed as she danced. She smeared them across her face, deliberately ruining her makeup, the distortion adding just another digression to their strange, intimate conversation. And there was joy, curiosity, discovery and love, celebrated and forbidden. Together, they stood in awe of the wondrous pyramids of New Spain and Granada, falling into a swarm of bodies, limbs all reaching for the next great pleasure. It was a travelogue, a trip through time, an orgy of spirits and hearts, and it united their minds in ways Alex had never experienced.

He had never desired Joanna, at least not physically. Admired, yes, but this was so much more than either emotion. He felt a creature wrap around his leg, binding it to hers and knew it was a snake unlike any in nature, its touch warm and comforting in all its strangeness. It bound their naked bodies together in pure, platonic joy, celebrating curiosity's promise—Lucifer's promise—fulfilled.

Despite his anticipating Joanna's every movement, she was no one's puppet, commanding each motion with independence and determination. He wanted to turn to Jago, but his body refused. It wasn't Jago resisting him… it was Joanna.

Don't look away, Alex. Don't abandon me on this journey we've begun. Not until it's over.

He watched each movement capture their shared rage, sadness, joy, excitement and hope. Without words in their way, Joanna plucked them straight from his heart, which still beat an irregular rhythm, keeping pace with the dance. Occasionally, Joanna would let out another screech, or a laugh, or start singing in a language he didn't know. Was it the same language he'd heard at *La Otra Cava*? For the moment, *La Otra Cava* seemed no less real a place than this.

There was no build to a performative 'big finish' that would leave the audience spellbound. Alex felt the snake release his limbs, its warm flesh sliding off him to find new creativity elsewhere. Joanna remained, wrapped in his arms in their shared mind's eye. Vicente spooned her from behind, while Jago did the same for Alex, four naked bodies that at last rolled over, splayed north, south, east and west like the cross, staring wide-eyed and innocent as virgins at the same god to which Joanna had offered their dance.

And then, she stopped. Standing on the stage, hair hanging low over her face, drenched with perspiration, she took her bow. Alex at last saw Jago smiling, while Maria stood from her seat, her eyes wide, hands over her mouth. The music faded and they waited, until at last Maria turned to him.

"You can have any nights you want." With no further explanation, she retreated, making it as far as the house doors before Jago spoke.

"Thursday," he said, as if this required no further clarification.

Maria nodded. "Easily done. I'll make sure *Alice's Wild Trip* is bumped out on time."

"*Alice's Wild Trip?*" Alex asked. "Really? He's going with that title? Does Disney know?"

"You can have Si-Man's entire run, opening on the Thursday."

"No, *just* the Thursday," Jago said again. "One night. Opening and closing."

Vicente emerged from the tech booth, while Joanna pushed the hair back from her face, tucking it out of the way into the back of her dress. They all stared at Jago.

"Jago?" Alex asked. "I think we need to discuss this."

Maria put her hands on her hips. "Look, I'm a busy woman. Your new show is brilliant, but make up your minds. Are you sure you just want—"

"Just Thursday," Jago repeated, turning to Alex with a confident smile. "Then, let them talk about nothing else for those two weeks. Let them all wish they'd gotten a ticket."

"This is stupid," Vicente snapped.

"Listen to your techie," Maria said. "If you don't take those two weeks, I'm stuck with Leo fucking Mendoza because he surely will, even if he has to make his parents eat the rental, and we can't strike his set for a one-night show. Alex, I implore you—"

"Two weeks, Maria. We'll take it. Thanks," Alex said, exchanging nods with Joanna and Vicente. Only once Maria was gone did he turn to Jago. "Only one night? After all this? Are you mad?"

"Not in the slightest," Jago answered, eyes bright as he fixed them on Joanna. "Tonight was excellent, yes? A taste of what you can create together. But can you do the same every night? For two weeks? What do you intend to do next time?"

"Good question. Alex, do you have notes for me?" asked Vicente.

Alex knew Vicente well enough to tell when he was biting back a sarcastic comment. But he'd been so caught up in Joanna's performance, he'd taken none. "I… no. Sorry, Vis, I… it was perfect."

"*Perfect?* Okay…" His friend hesitated. "I just can't promise it'll be the same every time."

"Exactly," Jago said, "and it never will be again." Without another word, he approached the stage, where Joanna sat cross legged, smiling serenely as if the dance hadn't ended.

Alex followed, not taking his eyes off her. "Are you all—?"

"Alex," she said, holding up a finger to shush him. "You of all people know I am more than 'all right.'"

He turned to Vicente, who'd joined them. "How much of the lighting did you write down? Maybe I can fill in the gaps or make notes from memory."

"I didn't write anything down," Vicente continued before Alex could make a sound. "I know what you're thinking. I just knew how to wing it. Don't ask me how. It was like we shared a mind. Jo?"

Joanna hummed with satisfaction, articulating nothing.

"I think this is a discussion you three need to have," said Jago with an air of resignation. "Alex, I'll be outside. Walk with me when you're done, please."

"Excuse me? I think we all deserve to know why you only wanted this to play one night."

Jago shrugged. "You already know why. Because you'll never repeat what we just experienced. Every night is just one night."

"So, you're saying we've set ourselves up to crash and burn?"

"I said no such thing." Without elaborating further, Jago left them alone in the dark, silent theatre.

"He's right," said Joanna. "I don't know what just happened, Alex. It was like Vis said, sharing a mind."

"What did he do to us?" asked Vicente.

Alex shook his head, scratching at his palms. "Whatever it was, we need it. Maybe that's why we'll never repeat it. He's doing a runner."

"Darling, that doesn't make sense," Joanna observed. "He's waiting for you outside. *You*, specifically. That doesn't sound like a runner to me."

Alex had to admit this was not the act of someone leaving them high and dry. In fact, besides the odd insistence that they perform only one night, Jago's every action and word had only brought out the best from their show.

Joanna stepped closer, kissing his cheek. "Even if he has some strange ideas, it's bad manners to keep a cute boy with your best interests at heart waiting."

"Vis?"

Vicente shrugged, caught between a damning opinion of Jago and an inability to deny their strongest performance yet. Before he could second-guess himself, Alex threw his arms around each of them, grabbed his knapsack and hurried out to meet Jago.

CHAPTER TEN

The line for San Ginés chocolatery resembled the bread queues they'd seen in photos of Russia or Romania, snaking around the corner, along the Pasadizo.

"Bloody hell," Alex said. "I hope you aren't proposing we get churros?"

"We can if you like. Don't worry, you're just seeing San Ginés from another time. Once the magick passes through you, it's impossible to tell what residual effects might linger. In my case, visions of the past or the future were common. It stands to reason you might see the same."

Alex stared at the river of people in casual fashions that would have stood out for all the wrong reasons among the fashionistas that haunted Chueca. "It's sure as fuck not the Franco years."

Jago gripped his hand, then smiled as this simple act appeared to allow him to share Alex's vision. "You're right. Twenty-first century, I'd say."

Alex's gaze fell on a young woman holding one of the many illuminated rectangular discs that anyone in line not talking to their friends seemed to be holding. She tapped at it with bored indifference, pushing her thumb along the glowing surface as if in search of something. "What on Earth are they doing?"

"On the other hand," Jago said, guiding him down the hill toward the palace district. "Too much detail about the future can ruin one's connection to the present. It seems like we're both getting ahead of ourselves."

"You're telling me they're from the future? That there are people from the future, here in 1980, queuing for churros at San—"

"I said you're *seeing* people from the future. What you're seeing is perfectly real, it just hasn't happened yet. Seeing snatches of it here and there are fine. Just keep in mind, it can come from the past too. I saw a dinosaur once. That was a trauma."

"Jago…" Alex gritted his teeth. "*How?*"

"What happened in the theatre? Surely you didn't think that was just a three-way experience?"

Alex's mind drifted to the image of Vis spooning Joanna, Jago spooning him, and the human cross they'd formed.

"Exactly."

"You're reading my mind now?" Alex let go of Jago's hand, quickly looking over his shoulder to check if anyone had seen.

"Not unless you share it with me. What sort of busybody do you take me for? I told you, I'm a witch. I'm sure it won't surprise you to learn what happened in the theatre stems from that power. I'm more specifically trained as an Entropist. My powers lie in the manipulation of time, fate, and the paths it might take. And after you tap into those powers? You might see visions of tourists from the future, or great beasts or monuments lost to time." Jago shrugged. "Or you might see nothing at all. They're echoes of magick, nothing more. They won't hurt you. They can't even see you. Just don't go looking for them. Your brain won't like being tested in that way."

Alex tried to gather his words as they rounded the block, and the lights the Royal Palace emerged. The largest palace in the world still in use, it gave the city one final burst of light and grandeur before the darkness of the monarchy's private hunting grounds, now a park for all to enjoy, stretched out for several miles below the ridge. "That's not how it felt, though. It was more primal and willful than that, like Joanna and I were in this weird mental conversation."

"Willful?" Jago took hold of Alex's arm, guiding him away from the palace, up the hill toward Plaza de España. "Perhaps you're savvier in the ways of Shapers than you think?"

"Shapers?"

"A fanciful term the more political among us use for themselves, shaping reality and whatnot. I'm more interested in that term you used. Willful? It carries some weight in Shaper circles too. It is commonly said that magick is divided by what is known and what is unknown, and by what is fated and what is—"

"Willed." It surprised Alex how much sense this made. "You mentioned politics? You mean there are more of you?"

"Too many. Personally, I'd rather limit my involvement." Jago gave him a wan smile, squeezing his hand. "I prefer to commit my energy and talents to people I care about. To art. To beauty."

"And what do you mean 'more savvy' than I think?"

"You felt that will to explore flow through you. What manifested on stage was a love letter to discovery and curiosity. A pardon for Eve, perhaps? That would make a fine title, if you want to invoke fairy tales. These are natural concerns for a new initiate, but you'll grow bored with them quickly. And will your audience share them? That's the real test."

"Jago... I'm not a witch."

"You're right, let's not jump to conclusions. You may have simply tapped into my power, but honestly, Alex? The kind of connection that transpired between you and Joanna is something I'd expect of a Mentalist. In terms of the four schools of magick, they're our polar opposite, a magic that is known and willed. Entropy, on the other hand, stems from fate unknown."

Alex stared at him blankly.

"Are you keeping up? I can draw you a chart."

"I understand your... quadrants." He slowed as they passed the Cervantes monument, one of his favourites in the city.

Jago smiled at him as they admired the statue dominating the plaza. "Now, he definitely had it."

"Cervantes was a witch?"

Jago laughed, squeezing Alex's shoulder. "No, but he did know how to weave magick. It's that lightning in a bottle I described to you."

"Look, I don't know if I'm a witch or not, but..." Spying a cluster of broken needles at the monument's base, Alex dismissed a foolish thought that they might be overheard. "Do I have it? Don't tell me you don't know."

"Whether I know or not doesn't matter. I can't answer that, Alex."

"Jago, please?"

"If I tell you no, you'll give up and stop creating. You'll call yesterday a fluke produced by your connection to me and my magick, and we will have killed something beautiful. If I say yes, you'll spend the rest of your life beating yourself up over not being the next Cervantes or Lorca. Neither of these outcomes is acceptable. You're the man you are and the artist you are, and that is enough, at least for me."

Jago's lips were on his before he could say anything stupid, and they were more than welcome. They were warm, eager to forgive his doubts and flaws, and he could have allowed it to go on all night if he didn't need answers.

"Then why did you want us to close after just one night?"

"Have you ever seen lightning keep its brilliance for two weeks? Your play as it stands right now is a love letter to discovery and exploration, played out on stage through your willing vessel, Joanna. You'll get one hell of an opening night out of it, perhaps even a few nights' run. But by the end of two weeks? I fear your audience…"

Alex resumed their walk with a harrumph.

"Don't misunderstand me," Jago continued, catching up to him. "I'm not trying to belittle your triumph or get in your head.

What would I know, in any case? I'm here to support you, Alex, whatever you decide."

They paused again at the Fuente del Nacimiento del Agua, where Jago squeezed his hand again, leaned forward, and kissed him. Alex accepted it, hoping the purity of the sensation would sweep away the confusion, self-doubt, and anxiety now clouding his heart. It did nothing beyond tasting good and stiffening his dick.

"Nice to know I can still get a reaction from you."

"I'm sorry. My head's just…"

"Overwhelmed with discovery?"

"Is it dangerous? Magick, I mean."

Jago scoffed. "Sweet, lovely man, exploration's always dangerous." He pointed toward the illuminated windows of the palace. "To their ancestors—*our* ancestors, let's be frank—discovery justified wiping out entire nations. Greed justified the extermination of empires. Now, we walk streets paved with the blood of those empires, and there was a lot of it. Even Queen Isabella told Columbus to steady the fuck on once she learned the price of that wealth."

"I'm not sure a lecture on colonial sins is going to help me navigate this, Jago."

"Navigate what, exactly? Your latent powers, assuming they exist? Or are you hoping to understand *my* powers? All right, let's talk about the entropy of colonialism, since we're on a theme. God rolls the dice of history. Nation A destroys nation B and takes what it possesses. Now, what if this had happened in reverse? Would nation B have destroyed nation A, given the chance? For greed? Religion? Sheer cruel fun? All are human temptations, and all played a part in nation B's destruction as fate has played out for us. Now, let's jump forward a little way. Nation A—Spain, in case that wasn't patently obvious—has now squandered its ill-gotten gains and lost its once formidable place in the world. It falls into dictatorship a few decades later. Cut off, forgotten as the world goes to war, left to fight its own hellish dispute for a soul it has long lost. Perhaps this dictatorship is the nation's time in Purgatory? Perhaps the religions of the East are right, that Hell is merely a temporary state to clean one's karma before starting life anew. Let's be honest, if in the next century tourists are lined up around the block for churros at San Ginés, I think we're going to be okay." He cradled Alex's chin in his hands with sensual confidence, then put an arm around Alex's shoulder, pointing to the hilltop building on the other side of the gardens.

Alex shuddered, recognizing the Templo de Debod. The shallow waters that had drowned Si-Man reflected the moonlight, bathing the temple's shadow in a strange glow.

"You just never know when or where accidents will happen. What if he'd chosen not to be there at that time, in that place? Yet the poor fellow did, and his death grants us opportunity.

"That's cold, Jago."

"That's entropy, and you accepted it. It's neither good nor bad, simply fate. Like the death of an empire. Egypt falls so Greece can rise. It then falls to make way for Rome. Today, we celebrate them all. Creation grows wild in the compost of tragedy."

Alex eyed him cautiously. "Meaning what, exactly?"

Jago put his arm around Alex's shoulders, turning their backs on the temple and facing the palace, which rose in full illumination over the darkened gardens. "It's too beautiful a night for this."

"Jago?" When he got no answer, Alex slipped his arm off his shoulders and turned to face him. "You didn't... surely?"

A conflicted look filled Jago's eyes. "If you *are* one of us, then you're the one working the magick of will here, mister director, not me."

"Look, no more riddles!" Alex gripped Jago's wrist. "No more bloody metaphors or grand talk about lost empires or tourists from the future. What did you do, Jago?"

"You're hurting me."

"Sorry." Even as Alex let go of Jago's arm and backed away, he felt himself shaking. Whether it was with rage, fear, or the hurt of betrayal, he couldn't be sure. Perhaps a combination of all three, or perhaps none. "You owe me the truth."

"The truth of what? That Si-Man lost his footing on a bender, hit his head and drowned in a few inches of water in the shadow of an Egyptian temple? I hope for his sake that Anubis isn't a theatre critic."

"That's not funny."

"Can you possibly think me so malevolent? If someone meets their fate—whether it's a self-described artist or a hustler thieving wallets from unwary fairies on a night out—it *is* fate."

Paco, the hustler. Alex remembered the flashing lights, his fleeting glimpse of his broken body. "Jago? Look at me, please."

Jago turned his head, seeming tired all of a sudden. "I don't murder people, Alex."

The look on Jago's face all but crushed him, appalled that for all his pains to dissuade and deflect his questions, to explain the inner workings of a world to which Alex, in no small act of confidence, had been invited, it still had to be said aloud.

"I saw you both nights."

"Exactly. You were with me both nights. So why even consider such a thing, my beautiful alibi?" Jago took both of Alex's hands in his and kissed his fingers.

"Promise me, then. Put my mind at ease, if nothing else."

"Alex..." Jago gripped his hands tighter. "I promise you I didn't murder those two men. I also promise that I will have your back whenever you need me, for as long as you want me. And, if you'll let me, that means doing everything I can to make this damn show the best thing it can be, even over two weeks, if that's what you want. We'll make it happen somehow."

"Somehow?"

"I'm powerful, not inexhaustible. Whatever transpired between the four of us tonight to create what we saw..." Jago looked up at the temple again, as if its stones might reveal an idea.

"Inexhaustible? What are you telling me?" asked Alex.

Jago said nothing, rocking back and forth on his heels.

"Right. Forget it," Alex shook his head. "If it's that dangerous, we'll find another way."

"Is that all it takes for you to give up?" Jago at last smiled at him. "We'll make it work."

Alex shook his head, trying to do as he was told while Jago's revelations ran roughshod through his mind. "I just want this to be great, and I felt that for the first time tonight."

This time, their kiss was long, passionate, and exploratory, wrapped around one another with longing.

"Why, mister director," said Jago when their kiss finally broke. "Do you know how much fondness and admiration I have for you?"

Alex didn't know what to say, squinting as a car's headlights swept over them.

Jago put his hands on Alex's cheeks, drew him close and kissed him again. "I'll not rush you into feeling the same. Just understand that I don't lightly share what I shared with you. I know how I feel. That is enough for now."

Alex took Jago's wrists and lowered them gently, unable to disguise the worry lining his face. "But if recreating what happened tonight is going to exhaust you, *every* night? Jago, we can't do that."

"That's sweet of you to say, but remember, it might not be my power you're drawing from. If you are a fledgling witch, it could well be your own, meaning I'm more worried about how it's going to affect you. Two weeks of rehearsal, then a two-week run? That wouldn't be easy for either of us, to put it mildly. How many performances a week are you planning to have?"

Alex considered this as Jago stroked his jaw. It was a silly, almost condescending touch, but it carried such tenderness. "Is this the real reason you only wanted one night?"

"I am worried the novelty may wear off, and I do think remaining elusive has its benefits. But yes, you must also consider our durability as conduits. Frankly, Alex, I wouldn't do this *to you*."

If Jago had appealed to the temple's stones for an idea, it was Alex who received their revelation. The temple might still have creeped him out, still haunted him with conjured images of Si-Man's body face down in its waters, but his heart raced too quickly to be slowed by such doubts. Not anymore. "Then… no more rehearsals."

"Pardon me?"

"You said it yourself, it's better to have one glorious opening night than polished repetition. I can't speak for you, but what we just saw came from the most spontaneous energy I've ever felt in a theatre. So, that's what we do every night. No rehearsals, just live inspiration. Every night will be its own opening, and once people start to talk about it… Oh, Jago, can you imagine?"

"Alex, I'm not sure this is—"

"People will come back night after night after hearing what their friends experienced, until they realise no two performances are anything alike. Who else can truly offer that? An improv group? I'd rather gouge my eyes out."

"Alex, you're quite literally tempting fate into our shared minds for the sake of nightly dance. Are you ready for what that might do to Joanna and Vicente, never mind us?"

Alex caught himself pacing. Jago had a point, and Alex would be damned if he put Joanna and Vis at risk for a bloody show. "Okay, how's this? Three nights, Thursday through Saturday, six shows over two weeks. One performance each night, no encores, no matinees, no exceptions. Can we do it?"

Jago gave a slow, cautious nod. "I'd still feel more comfortable if I knew if it was my magick or yours powering the performance."

"Jago, we need at least that to break even."

"Let me take care of breaking even."

"What? No."

"Alex, let me share something I've learned from the greats. Artistic integrity does *not* allow room for pride when it comes to money."

"Seriously, it's too much. We'll manage."

"It's not too much. I'll wire it to you in the morning. Nobody else needs to know. See if you can bargain Maria down. She likes you, and you can pay your friends with what's left over."

Alex shook his head, at once floored by Jago's kindness, in awe of the strange powers they'd barely begun to explore, and disgusted at the way in which he'd thought those powers had been used. "Why?"

Jago took his hands once more and kissed him. "Let me walk you home."

Alex knew when his eyes were lighting up.

"Not…" Jago laughed. "I mean, yes, I'd like that too, but I have an early train in the morning."

"A train?"

"To San Sebastián… or Donostia, as the Basques call it. Some business I need to take care of."

"Here I thought you were going to gorge yourself on pinxtos and cava and laze by the sea."

Jago grinned, kissing his cheek again. "That would be an experience better shared, no?"

"Like the show?"

"Hah." Jago pushed a lock of Alex's hair off his forehead. "It is where fate has led us."

For much of their walk, Alex could not have asked for a better night. A breeze from the north swept away much of the heat that had stifled the streets. When they passed by San Ginés again, the queue of oddly dressed tourists staring into glowing devices was gone, replaced by the plump owner shutting up shop. They crossed Gran Via into Chueca, rounding two or three more corners before Alex saw Jago pause. A disdainful look crossed his face as he took measure of a poster for an upcoming exhibition at the Reina Sofia, showcasing Dali's early works. Before Alex could comment, Jago screwed up his mouth and spat hard at it, hitting Dali's image square in the moustache, bringing an almost comical sense to the artist's familiar, wide-eyed affect. Jago showed little satisfaction as he took Alex's hand again, and led them on.

Alex knew better than to ask. He waited until they were at his door before inviting Jago up one last time, knowing he would refuse. With one final kiss, Jago was gone, leaving Alex to climb the stairs to his apartment alone, contemplating where fate had led him. He tried to sleep, heating up some milk an hour later when he couldn't.

He flipped through the well-thumbed book of Lorca's poetry that sat on his coffee table. When it fell open to a photo of the poet on its inside sleeve, he almost dropped it, for there was Jago's face, smiling at him. He turned away, closed his eyes, tried to shake whatever sleepy fog his brain had accumulated and looked again. The face was almost the same. It was thicker and fuller, plumper in the cheeks. The teeth were less perfect, more that of a provincial man who put art before any vanity—the same Lorca he'd seen in a hundred photos.

He flipped on the television, only to see the grey bars that signalled the end of another day's programming on TVE. Beyond a couple of short naps on the couch, sleep eluded him. He tried to masturbate three or four times, only to have his mind replace the image of Jago's body with that of Vicente trying to drown Joanna, or Si-Man face down in the Debod pools. Each was a boner killer that, coupled with his exhaustion, made him nauseous.

His friends were fine, and Jago genuinely cared for him. He understood both those truths, and yet…

He returned to the kitchen, fixing himself coffee as the sun's first rays broke over Retiro Park. By eight o'clock, he felt human enough to pick up the phone.

Vicente answered, still groggy, but far from annoyed. "Hey."

"There's something I need to tell you, in person, as soon as you can," Alex blurted quietly. "And you're not going to believe it."

CHAPTER ELEVEN

"You're a witch?"

"No. At least… I don't know."

"But Jago's a witch?"

"You don't have to repeat it aloud." Alex adjusted his sunglasses as a jogger went by on the Paseo del Prado. "Look, where's Joanna? I told you to bring her."

"And I told you, she's not feeling great."

Alex scratched at the edge of the fountain where they were sitting, cursing himself for not thinking of this before. "Is she okay?"

"She's fine. When you guys didn't come back to the theatre— thanks for letting us know, by the way—we went up to Miguel's. Someone had scored hash and there might have been some angel dust there. I stuck to weed, but… anyway, Joanna's sleeping it off so she's in top shape for opening night. And will you stop being so uptight? You're the one half-dressed incognito. What are you? The Pink Panther?"

"Sorry. I barely slept last night."

"Mmmhmm?"

"No, Vis, we did not, and I thought you didn't like him."

"Right. I am also not that guy."

"What guy?"

"Who treats his ex like property and hates on every person they date, forever and ever amen until death do us both in. Besides, I like what he's done for Joanna and for you. What's he's *still* doing for you. Let's just leave it there. I'm not dating him."

Alex gave a series of sharp, sarcastic nods. "Oh, okay. And the witch thing doesn't bother—"

"Oh, come on, Alex. If I had ten pesetas for every weirdo I met into some freaky religion…" Vicente turned a fresh, unlit cigarette over in his fingers before snapping it in half and grinding it beneath his tapping foot. "You know this country missed the sixties, right? People are sinking their claws into all kinds of weird shit."

"I'm telling you Jago's not just some weirdo." Alex nodded to the foot. "You're doing well."

"Tell that to my nerves."

"Did you sleep okay?"

"Yeah, actually, like the dead. We both did. Of course, we skipped the coke, which probably helped."

"How do you two *find* these parties?"

"How don't you?" Vicente threw his head back, staring into the trees above and letting out an exhausted gasp. "You're living in party city and in case you haven't noticed, ding-dong, the Fascist witch, the *real* witch, is dead."

"You might want to ask Joanna what difference that makes to the Basques."

"You know we only ever hear about that from other people, right? Joanna knows who she is, no matter who thinks they're in charge."

"I know. Still an outsider, though. Just like I'm Andalusian. You're Galician."

"Are you trying to collect the set? Why'd you bring this up, anyway?"

"You brought up politics."

"Fuck," Vicente said, taking another cigarette from its pack and lighting it. "Okay, but so what if Jago's a witch or warlock or wizard or wanker or whatever the fuck you think he is? Are you going to stop seeing him?"

"He's away for a few days, in the Basque country—"

"Ignoring *that* slightly odd coincidence, Alex, that wasn't my question. Are you going to stop—"

"No, Vis, I'm not. Maybe. I… I don't know. I'm a little scared. I mean, I'm excited too, but…" Alex hadn't mentioned his suspicions about what had happened to Paco or Si-Man. That would have put Vis over the edge, sent him running from their project and maybe worse, from Alex's life altogether. "I need him, Vis. I don't know if it's for the show or what, but…"

With a slow nod, Vicente lifted the cigarette to his lips. "So are we waiting for him to come back before rehearsal, or—"

"We're not rehearsing, Vis."

"Say what now?" Vicente's face pulled back into an impish look of bemusement. "For a second, I thought you said—"

"No rehearsals, I mean it. What the audience sees will be what we create in the moment."

"Alex, that's fucking insane. We'll be closed after one night."

"Think about it, will you? What did you feel last night? How did you know what cues to hit? You're bloody good, Vis, but you're not psychic. Neither is Joanna, so how did she know what I was thinking and feeling so intimately she was able to manifest it on stage in an instant? We can't rehearse that, but I know we can do it again."

"Now you're scaring me. How, exactly?"

"Maybe through Jago? I mean, who knows what power he's got, really?"

"Or you?" Vicente asked with a smile, which vanished when Alex didn't smile back. He clapped his hands, sending a small tumble of ash to the ground. "Ignore me. I'm talking shit. So, you want each show to be spontaneous, *hoping* that whatever connected us… Man, if this fucks up…"

"It won't. Jago wouldn't do that to me."

"I hope you're right, *if* he's the one doing it. You're sure it's magick though? Come on, Alex."

"What do you mean 'Come on, Alex?'"

"Think of it like flamenco. Nothing's scripted. Nothing's rehearsed. They just turn up, start the rhythm and away it goes. After a while, they get so good at it—"

"I know how flamenco works, Vis. My grandmother—"

"Yes, I know the story. So, isn't that what we're doing? Perhaps that's how should we promote it? Psychic flamenco? Unless you're keen on the whole memorial for Si-Man idea."

Alex winced. "Might look a bit disingenuous, coming from us. And psychic flamenco sounds terrible."

"That's why you're the creative," Vicente answered, unoffended.

"I'll think it over. Maybe talk to Joanna. I think a title is the least of our problems right now."

"No kidding. If I understand you, you're suggesting we do a new show every night. Each one, improvised? Gutsy, man."

Alex nodded, trying to push the craziness from his mind. "Three shows a week."

"Only three?"

"Think about what we're asking Joanna to do. What we're asking of ourselves. Magick or not, it's intense, Vis. Besides, Jago's covering the theatre rental."

"Huh." Vicente took a drag of his cigarette, letting the smoke go with a low whistle. "Well, I can't accuse the guy of not being invested. Whether it's in you or the show, I'm not sure."

The athletic form of a hairy, shirtless young man distracted Alex as he jogged along the paths. He tilted his head to watch the square shoulders and powerful furry legs, separated by a flimsy pair of bright red shorts, disappear down the Paseo. Alex laughed as he caught Vis doing exactly the same thing. "I didn't think that was your type."

"I don't hate beards," Vicente said.

"As a gay man, I'm obliged to resist a possibly bi-phobic joke here."

Vicente laughed as he nudged Alex hard in the arm. "Arsehole."

"Thank you." Alex grinned, getting up from the fountain's edge, swinging his arms to stretch them and wishing he had half the jogger's confidence to remove his shirt. Fucking heat. "It's going to be great, Vis."

"Please, feel free to put that out into the universe as many times as you need to."

Alex wasn't sure he needed the universe. But Jago? Oh boy, did they need Jago.

CHAPTER TWELVE

"Alex, congratulations."

"There's still an hour until curtain, Maria." Premature or not, it was nice to have her confidence. She did scrub up nicely in the boyish, slicked-back haircut and bolero jacket she donned for openings.

"I know, I know. But I've every confidence in what I saw. I trust rehearsals went well? Smart of you to keep their location a secret, by the way. Where's your friend?"

Rehearsals? A secret location? Alex wondered what Vis had told her. "Joanna's backstage. Vicente's in the booth, getting ready."

"I mean your other friend. The strange one who wanted one-night-only?" She raised her vermouth and took a long sip. "Handsome, though."

After returning from four days in San Sebastián, Jago had indeed promised Alex he'd be there for opening night, and each night after that. Besides this, however, they'd met only twice, for a drink at Angel Sierra and for a stroll through the Prado. Both had felt shockingly mundane, with Jago deflecting all but the most superficial questions about witchcraft or his trip. They'd retreated to Jago's apartment after the night at Angel Sierra where, after several more glasses of wine on the couch, they'd crashed in Jago's upstairs bed. Their attempt at drunken lovemaking had ended with them snoozing in each other's arms. The mutual blowjobs they'd exchanged come morning were a far cry from Alex's first night in Jago's quarters. Jago hadn't even mentioned his witch's chamber, and Alex had been too polite to ask for an invitation, much less to try Jago's levitation trick again.

That *had* all happened, hadn't it?

In truth, Alex had been too fixed on tonight to mind. He'd spent more time with Vicente, who'd become a dance widower as Joanna immersed herself deeper and deeper into preparations. When she'd finally come out with Vicente at the end of the first week, Alex had asked her how everything was going, a question she'd avoided with that wan smile that had become so familiar to him. Vicente on the other hand had insisted she was eating well, sleeping well within her typical nocturnal schedule, and had never seemed happier.

Several times, Alex had tried to bring up his strange night at *La Otra Cava*, but as days passed, this encounter seemed more and more like a distant, macabre dream. Vicente, for his part, had experienced no more dreams, distracting himself with Alex and football in equal measure, including one tedious afternoon Alex spent watching one of Vicente's games, confirming his amicable divorce from the nation's one true religion. At least Vis had bought him drinks after.

"He *is* coming, isn't he?" Maria's voice snapped Alex out of his musings.

"Yes?" Alex glanced at the doors. Confidence, damn it. "Yes, he is."

"Can I fetch you a drink?"

"No, I'm fine. He'll be here soon, Maria, I promise."

"Promise?" She lifted the lipstick-stained glass to her lips again. "It's your show, not mine."

Alex excused himself with a wan smile. No longer able to stand watching the silent doors, he disappeared into the darkened theatre and into the tech box. "How's it going?"

"Hey," Vicente murmured without looking up. "I think we're all good, now. Do you think anyone actually saw Leo's show, even if they bought tickets? Because they fucked like hell with the lighting presets. I told you we at least needed a tech run."

"Of what?" Alex asked. "Jago says it's too dangerous to risk a connection more times than we have to."

"A connection? Is that what we're calling it now? Mind orgy has a better ring to it, surely?"

"Near traumatising foursome?"

"Now *that* would have been a title. Too late now, sadly."

Alex shrugged. "Maria says the guest list is full. If people show—"

Vicente was on his feet and hugging him before he could finish. "Let's focus on that first bit, okay? Guest. List. Is. Full. It's gonna be great, my friend. Si-Man's psychic advisor promised me that."

"Si-Man's psychic…"

Vicente grinned.

"You're going to Hell."

"Can't be hotter than in here. I'm going to get some water. Do you want anything?"

"Have you seen Jago?"

Vicente frowned at him. "You mean you haven't? He was backstage half an hour ago, talking with Joanna."

Alex let his jaw go slack before biting his lip.

"Look, umm…" Vicente shuffled his feet. "Maybe we should talk after the show?"

"Vis?"

"I'm sure it's fine. The guy's weird, we both know that."

"A witch? Weird?" Alex smirked. "Yeah, isn't he?"

They left the booth and went their separate ways, Vicente to the lobby and Alex backstage. He disappeared behind the flats they'd hastily repainted in the style of what Alex had always thought was one of Cordoba's prettiest streets. Blue flower pots dotted whitewashed houses, all standing out against a cloudless sky, a black cat weaving its way along a terrace. It was idealistic— cartoonish, even. Perhaps some pretentious Madrileño critic would tear him apart for it, but so what? Once the show started, there would be no argument. In this house, the dogs from Andalusia did the tearing.

He crossed the space that buffered the sound between the stage and the dressing room, trying to hide his nerves as he rapped on the door.

"Come in!" Joanna sounded positively overjoyed.

When Alex saw her, she looked even better despite her unblended makeup, glowing as if the spirit of the show itself had imbued her. Sitting next to her with a glass of red wine, Jago looked tired by comparison, sitting low in his seat, his white shirt unbuttoned almost to the navel while—miraculously—not showing a spot of red wine. He stood up, taking Alex in a warm hug and kissing both his cheeks.

"I'd offer the same," Joanna said, turning back to the mirror. "But I'm halfway done, and I fear I'd leave your shirt looking like the Shroud of Turin if Jesus was a drag queen."

"To date, we've little evidence that he wasn't," said Jago. "How's it looking out there?"

"Empty so far, but Maria says the guest list is full, so… Where the hell have you been?"

"Here." Jago stared at him blankly as if this were a complete answer to the world's most obvious question. "Sorry, I meant to come find you, but by the time you arrived, we were deep into our conversation."

"Jago's been telling me marvellous things about his trip." Joanna grinned, blending her rouge. "Been making me quite homesick, if I'm honest. Have you been to Zugarramurdi, Alex?"

Alex noticed Jago's face darken, if only for a second. "Never heard of it."

"We should go, the four of us, together. I've heard about the Basque witches, of course, but I've always dismissed those stories as the church being the church when it came to opinionated, inconvenient women."

Jago gave them both a patient nod. "The history's quite real, I assure you. Most of it, anyway. The fire caves are something to see."

"Fire caves?"

"Most caves are shaped by water. It's said that to be imbued with magickal properties, they must then be refined by fire." Jago turned to Alex with a smirk. "It's not as if I've witnessed the process first-hand."

"I thought you went to San Sebastián?"

"I did. I hired a car from there. The historic centre of Basque witchcraft isn't exactly a hot tourist destination, you know? There's no train." Jago raised an eyebrow, as if reading every question that passed through Alex's mind. "I'll tell you more over a drink."

"Fine," Alex conceded, checking the time. Thirty minutes before curtain. "Will you excuse us? I'd like to talk to our star."

"*Our star*," Joanna said, mouth wide, fingers splayed at either side of her face like Gloria Swanson in *Sunset Boulevard*. "You say the sweetest things, Alex."

With a polite nod and a kiss on Alex's cheek, Jago retreated, closing the dressing room door behind him.

"Can you pass me my wig?" Joanna asked, fixing her skull cap as Alex complied. She picked up a brush and went into battle with it. "I don't know how this thing gets so bloody knotted every time it's moved. It's a straight wig."

"Nothing in Madrid is as straight as you think."

"Tired, but true."

Alex took the seat Jago had vacated, moving his unfinished glass of wine out of accident range. "How are you feeling?"

Joanna grinned. "Exhilarated. Aren't you?"

Alex smiled over a breathy, forced chuckle. "I mean, this is not what any of us signed up for."

Joanna turned to him over the edge of her chair. "Darling, this is no reflection on you, but what we signed up for was going to suck. I don't say that lightly, but this?"

"This?"

She shrugged, straightening the last tresses of her wig with obvious satisfaction. "We all saw and felt the same thing. I'm excited to feel that again, aren't you?"

"Of course. I just wish we knew more about how it worked."

"Don't we? It's witchcraft, isn't it?"

Alex hadn't been ready for quite so much frankness. "Umm… is it?"

"Really, Alex? Playing dumb doesn't suit you. You start dating a witch, he starts coming to rehearsals, and the whole damn show catches fire in the best way, like something I've never experienced on stage."

"I suppose Vis filled you in, then?"

She looked up at him, momentarily hurt. "Vis didn't say a word. You told *him*, but not me?"

"I asked him to bring you along." Alex shrugged, unsure what else to say as Joanna stood up and took her dress off the rack. "Look, it doesn't matter."

"Hmmm, you're forgiven. But the improvisation? No rehearsals? Jago's trip? It didn't take much to put the pieces together, though it did spoil the game a bit when Jago told me."

"He told you?"

She nodded. "To be fair, I asked. He didn't seem caught off-guard or offended, though. He seemed more impressed, if that doesn't sound like I'm bragging."

"And this doesn't bother or scare you?"

"Why should it? I know what I'm feeling on that stage. I understand why you cut us down to three shows a week, at least until we know what we're playing with. But I'm on the cusp of something wonderful here, Alex, thanks to that man." She tilted her head toward the door, reaching to fasten her dress. "Help do me up?"

Alex waited for her to turn around, fastening two elusive clasps on her dress.

"Thanks." Satisfied, Joanna turned around and gave him a kiss on the cheek. "Now go let him work his magick on you. We've got an audience to wow."

"What makes you think I'm not working my magick on him?" Alex said with a grin, picking up Jago's wine and leaving her to finish getting ready.

When he closed the dressing room door, Jago was waiting, leaning against the wall in a dark corner, arms folded over his chest, watching Alex with smug satisfaction.

"You forgot your wine," said Alex.

"Our wine." Jago wrapped his hand around Alex's under the glass.

Alex smiled as they raised it together. "To psychic flamenco."

"To what?" Jago laughed.

Alex took a long sip. "Something Vicente said. I thought it was funny."

Jago lifted the wine to his lips and finished the toast. "I'm glad you didn't call it that. Though *Dogs of Andalusia?* I don't know whether to be honoured or offended. I hope Dali and Buñuel don't sue."

"I doubt that. I didn't know what to call it. Joanna suggested *The Bitch of the Basque Lands*, but I thought that would get us into even more trouble."

"Next time, when you have a faithful audience."

"I don't know. Next time I thought we'd go for something really silly, about a boy that works in a café? Maybe we'll give him a seagull's head?"

"Dear gods," Jago pinched the bridge of his nose. "You are—"

"Stirring you up." Alex took the wine back and drew another long sip. "I'm just happy, is all. Though I would have liked you to at least check in with me before talking to Joanna."

"Yes, bad manners, I'm sorry." Jago kissed him, squeezing his shoulders as he withdrew. "I'm just happy you're happy. That means everything. But you have an opening night public to schmooze."

Alex winced. Seeing Jago in that smart white shirt with red swirls embroidered on it, atop black leather trousers? Schmoozing had little to do with what he felt like doing, and their public had even less. "Be my date?"

Jago stared at him with surprised delight. "I would not have been so bold as to ask."

Alex took him by the hand, leading him out of the theatre.

*　　*　　*

Alex had been glad of Jago's hand as they'd weaved through the genuine well-wishers, the rubberneckers, and the jealous pricks who'd come hoping to watch them fail. Leo Mendoza fell into that last category, but Alex had smiled and accepted his congratulations with a frosty hug while Jago checked for knives in his back, or so they joked once Leo was out of earshot.

Vicente, who hated these gatherings, remained in the theatre. Alex wondered if Joanna had allowed him access to her dressing room, or if he'd been brave enough to request it. Maria had introduced Alex to several people sporting loud jackets and louder rouge whose names he promptly forgot, then abandoned him once it was clear Alex—or the cute item on his arm—could draw a crowd for himself. He wanted another glass of wine. Or six.

The four who'd breakfasted at Café No Mismo the morning after Si-Man's death had snuck in at the last moment, though the director, Red Jacket, perhaps eager to avoid recognition, had shown up in dowdy drag, and might have been quite anonymous had the other three not dressed in much the same fashions as they had that morning. He offered Alex a knowing look in the lobby, which Alex took as good luck.

The theatre opened. The audience took their seats. Vicente gave the nod from the booth before Alex took his seat next to Jago.

"Ready to make magick?" Jago asked, grasping his hand.

Alex's nerves denied him so much as a quick, sarcastic remark. The evening was going better than he'd dared hope. The crowd hushed, the house lights dimmed, and the same strange music that had haunted them at their impromptu audition filled the auditorium. Jago's hand grew warmer, its softness wrapping around Alex's wrist, until he felt the steady rise and fall of a man's chest under his arm. Like a double exposure, he watched Joanna take the stage, each sweeping movement another sound in a language of male-on-male lovemaking in which she, to Alex's knowledge, should not have been fluent. But fluent she was, as the handsome, dark figure of a man vanished his cock in one confident swoop of his lips.

Gasps from the audience ranged from scandalised to excited to titillated. Yet this was no pornography on stage. This was Joanna pouring herself into the dance and finding movements for words dubbed obscene for all that made them beautiful. Alex was vaguely conscious of two or three walkouts, but he was too wrapped up in the performance to be sure, much less care.

Joanna played the scene until both men teetered on the brink of climax. Then, with one dramatic sweep of her arms, and a scream so full of joy it might have revived the dead for a second go-around, they came.

All of them.

Alex hadn't even realised he was hard, and was relieved when his pants remained dry. But the groans, cries, howls and gasps that passed through the audience as eighty-four semi-simultaneous orgasms erupted through the crowd like a string of firecrackers would surely haunt his nights for months to come.

Then, another gasp as the reddened, sweat-soaked face of the man who'd come with his lover within the confines of their story filled their minds—the modest, playful, grateful face of Federico del Segrado Corazon de Jesus Garcia Lorca.

This time, Alex was sure of at least five people walking out… and one screaming.

The music shifted, and Joanna progressed to the next movement. Anxiety and a fear of discovery now replaced all horny sensuality. It was clear from the clothes that their story was a period piece, full of 1930s peasants in drab, dirty dress, interspersed with military men wearing hard, cruel expressions. The nervousness that overtook Alex wasn't for them, however. A poem. Joanna's dance now spelled out the cadence and rhyme of a poem. The anxiety of its near-completion gripped the audience in its collective gut, not knowing how they could read into the dance so clearly but unable to deny the sensation that unified them. It was a fear every actor, every director, writer, musician, painter, sculptor, poet, designer … every human who'd ever attempted to put anything into the world knew all too well. The fear of their work not mattering. Of being forgotten.

Lorca's image blended with Joanna's again, as she sat down on the stage, accepting the embrace of the man who'd so pleased Lorca—and the audience—in his bed moments before. The man caressed them with such assuring gentleness that the anxiety gave way to sadness. Alex, along with every soul in the audience, remembered chances missed for fear of failure—songs, stories, and images that had longed with such urgency to be shared, only to be shamed into obscurity, a private joke never told or a song never sung, and behind each one, a memory that had meant so much more than a lost piece of art.

Joanna became the poem, filling the auditorium with such joy and hope, it was as if she'd reminded them—as if *they* had reminded them, for Alex was no longer sure where Joanna and her movements ended and the characters in their story began—why they'd chosen to be the person they were. They would make any sacrifice necessary to share their songs, stories, poems, and pictures; perhaps even life itself.

Kindness, relief, laughter, irritation, the bitter words of an argument... Joanna had a move for all of them, each one transforming as it reached the audience in a form they saw so clearly within themselves and those they loved; notions of family, born and created, notions of loyalty and betrayal that only poetry— or in this case, dance—could articulate.

A hush fell over the audience as anxiety returned, along with the military men who were this time, doubtless its cause. But there would be no hiding. No chance of escape. Thoughts of friends fled to France, Britain, or across the Atlantic fleeted through an audience now shifting in their seats. There were no images of Lorca as Joanna darted from shadow to shadow, stealing every opportunity to speak and to read in a dance that required no translation. By the time Lorca's face returned, it was staring down the barrel of a dozen guns, including one wielded by the man who had brought him such sensual satisfaction.

Screams pierced the darkness as the men fired, and Joanna and Lorca fell to the ground as one. Alex didn't know if it was shared knowledge, but as the lights faded, he knew who'd fired the bullet that had stricken Lorca's heart.

Gentle clapping broke the silence, growing rapidly into rapturous applause. By the time Vicente brought the lights back up on Joanna, the entire audience was on its feet, cheering. Joanna took her bow with steady grace, before beckoning Alex and Jago to join her. Jago held back, releasing Alex's hand and allowing him to own the surreal moment. He took the stage, acknowledging the audience with a deep bow before yielding the spotlight back to his star. Only now did Jago join him. Then, they threw the audience's love to the tech box, where Vicente accepted it with his customary stiff shyness. Yet terror gripped Alex as the applause died down and all eyes returned to him. He hadn't prepared a speech.

A panicked glance was all it took for Jago to jump to Alex's rescue. "Ladies, gentlemen, and persons of immaculate ambiguity…" A light chuckle and several cheers went through the crowd. "Thank you so much for coming. It has been a delight to see and feel hearts and minds that are so open." Jago shot Alex a sly wink. "And I'm pleased to say, so is the bar."

They escaped under the sound of more applause.

Jago grinned at Alex before stepping away. "Go own your night."

Before Alex could ask why Jago needed to go backstage or speak to Joanna again, he felt a hand on his shoulder.

"Darling!" Maria's voice was undeniable.

For the next twenty or thirty minutes—Alex couldn't be sure—the introductions flowed as free as the cava. He stopped trying to remember them after ten minutes or so, instead letting Maria, who, now sure of a hit, made certain to introduce him to every guest with semi-flexible purse strings.

"Alex?"

"Vis, thank God." Alex wondered if he'd said this aloud as he excused himself from a conversation to which he'd felt little more than an accessory and fell into Vicente's arms. "We did it, I suppose?"

"We absolutely did. And I'm fucking dying for a piss."

"Umm… so go? I think you've earned one."

Vicente shook his head. "It's a disco dispensary in that bathroom right now. If Maria wasn't so busy running you like a race horse, she'd be furious."

"Hey, if it gets us money—"

"I hear you. So, are we going to talk about what that was in there?"

"What what was?"

Vicente's brow darkened.

"Alex! Come, have you met—"

With that, he was back on patron's row. He'd expected his opening night to be full of Chueca bohos, queers and weirdos, not bored Los Geronimos widows looking to drop some liquid assets on the latest nonbankable discovery. At least it had kept Leo out of his hair.

The shrill blast of a police whistle silenced the evening's revelry for only a second before the murmurings of panic began. Whoever had brought the drugs didn't seem to matter now. They'd since dispersed through at least half the audience, who in various stages of inebriation or high, were now sobering up just enough to realise the implications of the black boots and uniforms now weaving through the crowd. The sound snapped Alex out of his fugue all the same, at least enough to follow when Vicente grabbed has arm and pulled him back into the darkened theatre and backstage.

"Come on, man! We need to go!"

"What? Vis? What's going on? Why are the police here?"

"Never mind that."

"Never mind—"

"They're gone, Alex!" Vicente propped him up against the dark wall, shaking him just hard enough to stir his attention. "Forty minutes, now, I haven't been able to find them and now I know why. He took her."

"What? Vis, you're not making any sense."

"Joanna!" Vicente barked again. "Your boyfriend? He's taken Joanna!"

CHAPTER THIRTEEN

With no small difficulty, Vicente had smuggled Alex out the back, then maneuvered his languid form into a taxi and taken them to his apartment, where he'd left Alex on the couch with a glass of water and a cup of black coffee for another forty minutes before returning. Alex, meanwhile, had taken one sip of the coffee and thought better of it, but as lucidity proved increasingly slow to return, he stomached more, trying to parse what Vicente had said. What their show had been. Why the cops had shown up at the theatre. He couldn't remember Vicente getting him into the car.

"Vis? Where are we going? Do you even drive?"

"Just chill, will you? I need to concentrate. It's Miguel's car, and yes, I drive."

"Let me rephrase that," Alex said. "Are you licenced to drive?"

"Who's going to pull us over between here and the Basque country at this time of night?"

"The Basque country?" Alex's head suddenly seemed clearer. "There's a damn good chance the police will, and they don't like insurgents, Vis."

"It's a good thing we're not insurgents then. Christ, Alex, I am nervous enough. What is wrong with you?"

The wine, thought Alex. Had Jago drugged the wine? *Our wine*, indeed.

"Look, where are we going? Why? What makes you even think—"

"Let's take those one at a time," Vicente answered through gritted teeth. "One, we're going to San Sebastián."

"San Sebastián? I'm really not in the mood for a seaside holiday, Vis."

Vicente struck his palm against the steering wheel, but otherwise contained his anger. "It's a place to start. You said Jago went up there for business not long ago? Well, I'm willing to bet that business had something to do with tonight. He's been planning this, Alex. Don't tell me he hasn't."

"Planning…?

"Oh, come on, man. He gets all over you and turns your head to get access to her?"

"If all he wanted was access to her, then why wouldn't he get all over you?"

Vicente shook his head. "Too close, maybe? Afraid we'd work out what he was doing? Maybe he saw he had an 'in' with you or he just fancied you more? How should I know? Fuck! I don't even…"

"What is your plan, Vis?" Alex asked, trying to keep the anger out of his voice now. "Once we get to San Sebastián, how do you intend to find them? Ask around?"

"I don't know. The hotels? Restaurants? Guy who looks like Lorca, only a hottie, thought to be in the company of local looking woman? It's not a big city. Somebody must have seen something."

Alex drummed his fingers on the ugly brown leather upholstery of his seat. "Yes, someone must have… but not in San Sebastián."

"Where, then?"

"Zugarramurdi!"

"Zugga-whatty?"

"The witch town. That's where he's taken her. And I'll bet it's to the caves she talked about."

"I…" Vicente shook his head again, driving on faith. "Glove box."

"What?"

"Miguel said he had some maps in the glove box. What? You think, driving in the dark, that I know how to get to this town I've never even heard of?"

Alex opened the compartment and rummaged through the promised maps until he spied one covering Navarre and the French border. He unfolded it across his knees. "I can't see a damn thing, Vis."

Vicente reached above their heads and flicked on the light. "Jesus, if anyone's going to pull us over, it's going to be now."

"Here!" Alex pointed to a small spot on the map within spitting distance of the French border.

Vicente peered at it, then turned out the light. "Okay. You'll still have to direct me. Next question. Why? I don't know, man. You tell me. I thought this guy was crazy about you."

"He's definitely not crazy." Alex gritted his teeth, still not quite able to believe Vicente's theory. "Maybe Joanna went willingly?"

Vicente's head spun with a glare that made Alex afraid he'd crash the car. "Without telling us?"

"I just mean, they were talking like old, best friends right before the show. That's how I found out about Zugarramurdi. That's where Jago's business took him, though to be honest, he seemed annoyed when Joanna mentioned it."

"Ahah, see? *There*. Right there, Alex. He seemed annoyed because he didn't want us finding out, perhaps? Free will? I don't think so. And even if she did, why didn't they tell us where they were going? No, man. Willing or not, this is way beyond fishy."

"Okay, okay! We'll find them, Vis. I promise. Next?"

"What?"

"Next question?"

"I don't know. Maybe..." They exchanged worried glances as the car's headlights lapped up the endless trail of road markings, catching the odd reflector as they went. "What are we going to do when we get there?"

"How long do we have to work that out?" Alex asked.

"I don't know. Without stops, five hours? Maybe six?"

"That gives us five or six hours to come up with a plan," Alex said, hoping to whatever god of fate would listen that the best course of action would be to do nothing at all.

*   *   *

No plan emerged.

Any trace of an idea that might have yielded a plan remained as obscured as the trail beyond their headlights as they swung into the spot where a few rusty signs promised they'd find the Zugarramurdi Witch Caves.

"Did you bring a flashlight?" Alex asked.

"No. Weirdly enough, this is my first time driving halfway across the country in the dead of night to stop an abduction. There may be one or two details I forgot."

"We don't know that it's an—"

"*Whatever it is, Alex!*" Vicente sighed, looking sheepish. "Sorry, I'm exhausted."

"It's four in the morning and you've been driving." Alex put a hand on his wrist. "Vis, they're going to be okay and so are we."

"They?" Vicente shook his head. "I'm sorry, Alex, but your new boyfriend isn't the one I'm worried about." They got out of the car and began following the trail downhill. Vicente cried out from in front as he stumbled. "Watch yourself. It's steep here."

"Thanks. Can you not break an ankle?"

"Mine or someone else's? Forget I said that, sorry."

Alex didn't bite. He knew Joanna's safety was Vicente's only concern, and if Jago had hurt her in any way, it would be his as well. But damn it, they'd shared minds—perhaps more. Surely if Jago had meant them harm…

"Over there." Vicente pulled Alex close behind a bush and pointed to the flickering fire that illuminated a far corner of the immense cave.

Alex couldn't see Jago, but he could make out Joanna clearly enough, sitting cross-legged in her white stage dress, staring into the flames, hair hanging low over her shoulders. "We need to get closer."

"No shit. How do we do that without being seen?"

"Vis?" Alex didn't know how he knew. He couldn't see Joanna's expression, nor the smile that he was sure had crossed her lips. It was perhaps fairest to say he felt her beckoning them, in the same way he'd felt her during the rehearsal and the performance. "She's calling us."

"*She?*"

Alex held out his hand. "Trust me?"

With plain scepticism, Vicente accepted Alex's hand. Together, they followed the rest of the trail, which widened into the enormous mouth of the cave. Now, Alex could see Joanna, sitting opposite an equally bare Jago. Except Jago lay supine on the other side of the fire, still as a corpse except for a steady intake and outgoing of breath.

"Come," she said aloud. "Don't be frightened, please."

"Frightened?" Alex asked as they climbed up the rocks to the outcropping where Joanna—he presumed—had built her fire. "Why should we be frigh…"

He had glanced behind him for less than a second, less time than it had taken Orpheus to condemn his love with the same action, yet what he saw chilled him as he held his breath, trying to will away what had to be an illusion. Hundreds, perhaps thousands of faces, mostly young women, though with an undeniable sprinkling of men in their number, dressed in archaic clothing stared back at him. Flaming torches illuminated their faces, many of which were scarred with puncture wounds, deep gouges or worse. Some were missing eyes or ears, others were burned beyond recognition. Yet all were staring at Alex and Vicente, intruders in their sacred place.

"Confused?" asked Joanna. "Perplexed? Fascinated or perhaps enticed, just as Jago enticed you?" Her hair shifted as she tilted her head. Alex noticed Vicente's hand tighten around his.

"My god…" Vicente said, looking around the cavern.

"God isn't here. Not the one you mean, anyway." Joanna rose to her full height, rounding the fire anti-clockwise until she stood before Alex. Her dress fell from her shoulders, leaving the fire's light to lick her bare skin.

"Jo?"

"Disrobe," she said quietly.

Alex didn't know what faith compelled him to obey, but he did. Ignoring their unexpected audience, he shucked off his shirt and began unbuckling his belt as if they'd become obstructions to his understanding Joanna's intentions, or the nature of this place.

Though he didn't interrupt, Vicente watched Alex in a way that made it clear this revelation had been Alex's alone. Once he was naked, Joanna gathered his clothes along with her costume, held them briefly to her face, then threw them in the fire.

"Jo! What the—"

"Vis," she interrupted him with a bored inflection that unsettled Alex. "You're a good man. But we've no more to offer one another."

Joanna snaked her arms around Alex's neck, kissed his face and languidly suckled his throat, chin and earlobes, all the while pushing her body closer to his. Yet Vicente remained as still as the Lucifer under which they'd watched her dance. Alex felt his cock stiffen, though nobody had touched it. It cast an obscene shadow against the cave wall, bouncing around in the fire's light as Joanna withdrew. Looking down with embarrassment, he saw firelight lap the smooth, tanned curves of Jago's body as his chest rose and fell. He too was hard, and the sight only heightened Alex's lust. Yet to cover or touch himself in any way seemed an act of sacrilege.

"Do you want to hold him?" Joanna asked. "I assure you, his hearts desire it."

"Hearts?" Alex asked. "Plural?"

Joanna retreated to the shadows and lounged against the stone, naked as Eve and silent as a grave.

"Alex," Vicente hissed. "We should leave."

Alex looked up at him, stunned by the suggestion. "*You* want to leave? Now?"

"Hold Jago," Joanna said again.

"Please?" Vis begged, shivering despite the fire. "Alex, this was a mistake. I'm so cold."

"My love?" Joanna's voice possessed no mockery, only the kindness and playfulness she had always shown Vicente during their time together. "Warm yourself by the fire. You must be tired as well."

Alex leapt to catch Vicente as his knees appeared to give way. He lowered him perpendicular to Jago, putting about three feet between him and the fire. Before Alex could ask if he was comfortable, Vicente was sound asleep.

"Joanna?" The name was thick with caution as he said it. "I don't know what you're doing here, but—"

"Why would you want to stop something you don't understand?" She returned to the fireside, sitting cross-legged once more. "Come."

Without a better option, Alex sat, trying not to look at the crowd or their penetrating stares. "Why are you here? Did Jago bring you?"

"We journeyed together. I think it's rather taken it out of him, though."

Jago and Vicente's long, steady breaths filled the silence between them.

"You drugged him," Alex said. "Was it the wine? Is that why I felt so—"

"You thought I needed rescue?" she asked. "How tediously chivalrous. Your imagination is better than that, Alex."

He swallowed as a young woman whose neck bore the dark outline of a rope bruise drew his eye. "I still don't understand. What are you doing here? The Zugarramurdi witches were just ordinary women who—"

"You needn't reassure yourself." She held up a delicate hand as she interrupted him. "They won't hurt you. But there is both truth and falsehood in what you say, and in the end, who's to sort the blameless from those with powers such as Jago's? They all gather here now, to these caves, forged in fire, to sup from a power that is as real as it is ancient."

Alex checked on Jago again, hoping that coming here hadn't doomed the four of them.

Joanna reached behind her, lifting a pot of ointment into the light.

"Is that what I think it is?"

"Our ticket here? As I said, we journeyed together, but he needs replenishment. Help me." She gave Alex a kind smile, procuring another pot and working the ointment into Jago's feet.

"What is it, exactly?"

"A flying ointment. Our dear friend and muse will need to take flight one last time before we're done here. Don't ask me what it's made of, just help me."

With no small hesitation, Alex massaged the substance into Jago's face, neck and shoulders, smearing more of it over his chest and arms, ensuring, just as Jago had when he'd done this to Alex, that every inch of his body was covered. For a brief instant, Alex wished he'd held his nerve the night he'd opened his eyes to find them hovering in mid-air, naked in each other's arms; that he'd embraced the experience and trusted what it could offer.

"Do you feel it drawing you closer?" asked a voice from somewhere deeper within the cave, neither male nor female, but a fusion of Joanna, Jago and… something else. "It's not too late, if you wish to be alone with him. My gift to you."

"Who's there?" Alex demanded. "Who are you?" He couldn't imagine letting Joanna out of his sight in that moment, much less making love to a man passed out.

The voice answered. "Of course… I understand."

"Show yourself!" His own voice echoed back at him. "What's going on, Joanna? Why are you here?"

"I simply had to know." She nudged Jago's genitals out of the way as she coated his thighs. "And tonight, I understood it with absolute clarity."

"Understood *what?*" Alex didn't know why he was hesitant to oil Jago's sex. It wasn't like he hadn't handled it before.

"What they wanted from me. What I wanted from them. You felt it, just as I did, in the theatre. Their story. Darling, he must be completely covered. I'm sure he'd rather you do it than me."

"Enough!" Alex pulled Jago's body against his, wrapping his arm around him protectively. "No more riddles or games or blasted metaphors. Who are *they?*"

"Darling, you saw for yourself. Lorca, and his last lover, the man who would become Jago."

Alex stared at her in disbelief.

"The man who killed him."

"I saw the show, Joanna." Somehow, he'd refrained from snarling. But real as it had seemed, their show was just a fine trick, blending magick, mischief, and strange poetry. "I don't know who that man was, but it was not *him*."

"But it was, in his last host. I don't know the fellow's name or how he came to join the Fascists. I've a notion he infiltrated them in secret, unwilling to let any other man kill his lover. What a terrible, romantic ending that would be. In any case, it's his secret to share, not mine."

"Joanna, this is…"

"A joke? A dream? No, Alex, it's a transfer. Tonight, there will be another. You felt their minds, shared as one, just as Jago shared it with me."

"Jago? He? They?"

"Both and neither. One and two, all at once. Now, oil his genitals, please."

"No."

"If you will not hear it from me, then spend these last moments with him." Joanna stood up, and before Alex could challenge or stop her, stepped forward into the fire, vanishing before Alex had time to scream her name.

Last moments? He held Jago tighter. Wake up, damn it. Wake up.

"Alex?" came Jago's voice from the darkness. The body he was holding slept peacefully.

"Jago? Where are you? Where's Joanna?"

"Alex, what she's telling you is true. I'm sorry. She caught me quite off-guard tonight."

Alex's body trembled as his frustration grew. "What do you mean?"

"I thought you were the one possessing magickal talent, but it was her. I suppose I should have known. She was… so different."

"Jago?" he asked, gathering his composure and lowering his voice, as if he could keep the audience from overhearing their conversation… assuming they heard anything at all. "What *exactly* are you?"

"I told you, a witch, like some of the souls here. Beyond that, Alex, I don't explain myself for fear of sending my companions mad."

"Just tell me!" he barked, unable to stop a sob from entering his voice. "You owe me the truth, at least."

"A muse? Perhaps it's as good a word as any. I was a simple weaver of magick when I found this creature and bound it to me. Over time, I have used its powers to delight and enrich souls across Europe and the East. More recently, in the Americas. I suppose Australia or Africa is the next logical step?" Jago let out a laugh as soft as a housecat's bell. "It started with the royal courts, then the common public, though I must confess, mass media in this century still overwhelms me. There's nothing quite like the intimacy of the theatre, don't you agree?"

"Jago, please talk sense."

"In simplest terms, Alex, I am both the witch and the creature in its service. Once I bound one being to my soul, it was easy to continue, and with each new bonding, we combine our talents. I come, I watch and listen, taking care to choose the right mind and heart. Feasting on lovely chaos, I bring out the very best they have to offer, releasing the creator they were always meant to be. When they can grow no further, we bond and seek out the next."

"Bond? You mean you… absorb them?"

"We merge, and from our composite parts, choose a desired form. Nothing sells talent like ideal beauty and charm, after all. But the illusion can't last forever. I can prolong the body's life, not immortalise it."

Alex looked down at Jago and was astonished to find the body of the great poet, Lorca, his hairline receding, portly belly overhanging his hips, and an undeniable smile warming his face. "You bonded with… This is Lorca's body?"

"The original, indeed, adjusted to suit our purposes. Alex, *I* am Lorca, just as I am the witch and the muse and every artist I have nourished over more years than I care to remember. Now, imagine if you'd done your *Blood Wedding*. No offence, Alex, but that would have been excruciating for me. Still, I wanted to be honest with you, so you saw the show you saw. Lorca was my lover, once. If I had simply murdered him in our bed, it would have raised questions, led the Fascists right to us. So I replaced a member of Franco's death squad. Once my bullet found Lorca's heart, it was a simple matter to 'disappear' his body myself."

The poet in Alex's arms smiled at him, opening his eyes at last, before returning to peaceful slumber.

"Were you also going to kill me?"

"I was going to offer you immortality. The chance to burn bright until your talent was extinguished, either by others or by your own doubts. Lorca found himself surrounded by enemies with no desire to flee. The only way to protect him was—"

"How convenient for you." Alex caressed his soft cheek and squeezed his shoulders. Not dead, but sleeping, just as Jago—if there was such a man—had been moments earlier.

"I preserve those talents for the next one I find, and the search is by no means easy. I've not met a worthy host since Lorca, someone whose talent and humanity I could love in equal measure. In truth, I wasn't there for you the night of the movie. I'd heard promising murmurs about the director. The singer, too, Alaska. But then I met you."

"Me?" Alex replied flatly. "You chose me over all the talent in that room?"

"You really must give up this unwarranted modesty. You possessed an energy I couldn't place. It made you easy enough to find, even that day at the protest. Then, I came to watch your rehearsal, and the true source of that energy revealed itself."

A cold shiver gripped Alex's body. "Joanna. You wanted Joanna."

"You said yourself she was the creative engine behind your show, and you were right."

Alex couldn't remember saying these exact words. "And me?"

"Don't misunderstand, we wanted you too. Lorca wanted your beauty. Your talent. Your kindness and loyalty to your friends.

Your charming self-doubt. All the usual business humans look for in a companion, at least if they're mad enough to date an artist. It all drew us to you."

"But my talent wasn't enough to be your next host?"

"Ah, *there's* that healthy ego. Don't worry, Alex. Artists beyond counting have gone on to very successful careers without my help. It's not so much that Joanna possesses a greater talent, but one I've not yet cultivated in all my years."

"Dance?"

"No. Magick as an art unto itself."

"Jo…Joanna's not…"

"Darling?" she said, rejoining them at last from the darkness. "I don't need your protection, but do me one favour. Take care of Vicente for me. He really does deserve a second chance, and it would be better if neither of your watched what's about to happen."

Alex scowled, shaking Lorca's body as if to rouse him, only to find Jago's athletic form in his arms once more. "Joanna, this is madness. You can't just *give* yourself to this thing."

"This thing you're holding in your arms like it's the broken body of Christ? This thing you happily went to bed with more than once?"

"That's when I thought he was human."

"He is many humans, and a great deal more."

Alex lowered Jago's head to the cave floor and backed away. "Come on, please. Let's go home."

A great sigh filled the cave as the entire assembled crowd drew breath. The sound rattled with death's final chill.

"Alex? Jago may have spared you this, but I won't. Do you think talent, opportunity, and beauty worth having comes without sacrifice? You saw the blood on our stage that day. You saw them take away that thief's body. You knew it when Jago made love to you and your bodies left the floor, and you knew it when Si-Man just happened to drown in shallow water." She tilted her head, like a teacher disappointed her student was playing dumb. "You accepted all his gifts. Now, I will accept his last one." Joanna kneeled at Jago's side, covered the last of his body with the ointment, and withdrew.

Alex bit his lip as the breath of the crowd found its own harmony, emerging as a long hum that filled the cavern like the organ of a cathedral.

"I could feel him searching for me," Joanna continued. "I couldn't reveal myself until I could make the transfer on my terms. Our audition for Maria was also an audition for him. As for getting certain obstacles out of your way, don't despise him for doing what you and Vicente could not."

Alex flinched as flames leapt from the fire between them and bounced off the cave walls. The entire chamber seemed for a second to glow hot with such light he had to cover his eyes. When he opened them again, Vicente was on his feet, standing perfectly still, head bowed and eyes closed. Alex watched as Joanna leaned close to Vicente's throat, whispering something in his ear. Like a sleepwalker, he stepped carefully behind her, putting his arms around her waist and resting his head on her shoulder.

Then, Jago began to rise from the cave floor, floating just as had the night he'd welcomed Alex to his witch's chamber. He grasped Alex's hand, at last opening his eyes and smiling. At the same time, Alex swore he felt hands take him around the waist, those warm, soulful lips on the back of his neck, sweet, orange blossom breath breaking over his shoulders. Jago's breath.

"Be everything we saw in you," Jago whispered.

The wind and the humming of the crowd picked up again, howling so loud and fast, Alex could no longer keep his eyes open. He felt his feet dragging forward over the stone, some irresistible force drawing the four of them nearer and nearer to the fire. His attempt to call Joanna's name met only silence as cave dust and ash whipped his ankles. He felt his naked body collide with hers, and the hot coals beneath his feet. What he didn't feel was the heat of flames curling his skin, like some mystic who had embraced them with no fear of being burned.

When Alex dared to open his eyes, a great light flooded them with such ferocity he'd no choice but to turn away, burying his face into a chest that was now Vicente's. His stage manager's black t-shirt caught Alex's tears as he tried against better sense to see what was happening to Joanna and Jago. It didn't surprise him that Vicente now stood behind him. It didn't surprise him to see Jago wrapping his arms around Joanna, or Joanna caressing Jago's shoulders and throat while they kissed.

It did surprise him, however, when she bit hard into his neck.

Jago's scream soared above the chorus and the winds, echoing against the cave walls and filling Alex's mind with dread. Joanna gripped her prey fast as she drank deeper and deeper, barely allowing a droplet of blood to escape her ferocious hunger. After several seconds of shock, a grin crept over Jago's face. It was meant for Alex, or perhaps for both Alex and Vicente. This… this was the power Jago had sensed. The power he craved. This was the next Jago, yet there was, Alex somehow knew, no way it could still be Jago, nor Joanna. Something new would emerge, and it would continue the witch creature's terrible yet wonderful cycle of creation anew.

"Alex?" Vicente whispered in his ear.

Alex pushed himself deeper into Vicente's arms, watching Joanna and Jago rise from the cave floor and disappear into the light, leaving a thin trail of blood in their wake.

"Alex," Vicente said again, kissing him on the neck.

Alex turned, taking Vicente's kiss deep into his mouth. He lifted Vicente's t-shirt up over head, pushing his face into his chest, welcoming the blond hairs that tickled his nose, that familiar scent of football, cigarettes and gentle musk that he'd so often inhaled with the ravenousness of a newly liberated young man in love. Vicente's pants slipped to the ground, and their bodies rolled together onto the stone. With each caress, each kiss, each touch and provocation, Joanna and Jago seemed as distant a memory as the play that had brought them first to this cave of witches, then back into each other's arms.

EPILOGUE

"Alex, darling, I know I've said it before, but congratulations!"

Excusing himself from his conversation with the film programmer from Sitges, Alex greeted Maria with a hug and a kiss on each cheek. "Thank you, I'm glad you liked it."

"So am I. You left us in quite a bind, last time, remember?"

"I said I was sorry, Maria. And the rental was still paid for."

"Yes, but imagine how much more we could have made with full houses. Besides, I love the look on your face when I bring it up." She winked at him over her the bubbles of her cava. "I must admit, after your 'one night only' dance event, I wasn't expecting a comedy about partner swapping."

"I just…" Alex shrugged, waving his half-finished wine in the air as he accepted a silent toast and a mouthed congratulations from Victoria, who stood at the bar pretending to listen to Peach. "I wanted to spread my wings, and I think I've had enough dance for a while."

"You *are* sticking around for the full run this time though, aren't you?"

"He is, yes," Vicente added, putting his arm around Alex and kissing him on the cheek. "We didn't put all this work in for just one night."

"Good. Now, let's just hope the censors don't shut you down."

Alex exchanged nods with one of their leads, the former White Rabbit whose package had certainly not let their show down. "If Broadway stars can flash their bits for thousands of strangers, I don't think our show's going to upset anyone."

"Not the new owner, in any case. She loved it."

Alex and Vicente frowned as Maria disappeared into the crowd, returning with a striking young woman on her arm. Alex and Vicente stared in silence, forgetting their manners until Maria coughed.

"Alejandro Vargas," Alex said quickly, extending his hand. "And our stage manager and director's assistant—"

"Vicente, I believe? Yes, I read your bios. Pleased to meet you." She accepted his hand. "You should be proud of producing work like this so young. If you and your colleagues can keep it up, we should do very well indeed."

"You're… the new owner?" Vicente got out, unable to mask his confusion.

"Forgive me. Isobel."

"Isobel?"

"Just Isobel." She smiled sweetly through bright red lips. "I'm sorry I can't stay for the festivities. I just wanted to congratulate you in person before I leave."

"Well, thanks again," said Alex. "Where are you going, if you don't mind me asking?"

"Istanbul at first, then I don't know. Perhaps Australia?"

"*Australia?*"

She offered them another cryptic smile and shrugged before downing her wine. "Congratulations again, boys. I'm proud of you."

Alex watched her pitch-black hair disappear through the crowd and out the theatre doors, into the night without escort. "Did she seem familiar to you?"

Vicente bit his bottom lip. "I can't place her."

"What she is, is extremely rich," Maria added. "Came into quite some money when her husband passed away just shy of forty, poor thing. No children. She's barely twenty-five, but says she's no urge to marry again. Just charity and theatre, including a generous stipend to this theatre." Maria clinked her glass against Alex's. "Which doesn't give you license to phone in a flop, mister director."

"I wasn't planning to."

"Good, because we'll need a new artistic director and programmer too. Something to think about."

The pair of them beamed until at last, unable to summon words, Alex took Vicente in a big, wet, celebratory kiss.

"I thought so," Maria said. "Now, if you'll excuse me, I'll let you boys enjoy your big night."

"Artistic director?" Vicente said.

"I…" Alex shook his head. "Oh my god, don't tell Leo. Not until I'm there to see it, at least."

"You're evil." Vicente grinned, kissing him again. "And I love you."

Alex took Vicente's hand, watching the crowd swarm their four-piece cast as they posed for photos.

"So, what do we do after this?"

"I don't know. Something about vampires?"

"That sounds ghastly. Nobody's going to go for that."

"I know. I was joking."

"Thank the gods. But I meant, what do you want to do tonight?"

Alex shrugged as flashes lit up the foyer. All eyes were on their squinting cast. "Disappear? Go home? Maria gave me a nice bottle of Valencia Bobal. I may have a few other ideas, if you're interested in workshopping them." He slid his thumb across the back of Vicente's hand.

Vicente kissed Alex on the side of his forehead, squeezing his shoulders. "That, mister director, sounds like a magic act worth catching."

HAUNTED HEARTS:
SEASON OF THE WITCH

Read all 11 books in the series:

https://mybook.to/HauntedHeartsTwo

Memories in Bone by J.P. Jackson

Heart of the Wren by Glenn Quigley

Currents of the Heart by M.D. Neu

I Will Always Find You by Ryan Lawrence

A Tall Cup of Joe by Matti McLean

Jade Lion and the Witch Boy by CD Rachels

Heart Shaped Wreckage by Shane K Morton

The Bairwick Witches by Eric David Roman

Andalusia Dogs by Christian Baines

Grayson's Magical Mishaps by Kevin Klehr

Riftwitch by Tal Frost

Acknowledgements

Thank you to all who've stared into the gaping maw of Queer horror and speculative fiction and said "more please." We have always been here, and you keep us here. Thank you!

Thank you to all my co-con-spirit-ors of the Haunted Hearts series for your encouragement, signal-boosting, inspiration, feedback, and determination to get our strange little collection out into the world.

Special thanks to my editor hex-traordinaire Jerry Wheeler, and to Glenn Quigley and C. D. Rachels for your early feedback and encouragement through drafting of the book. Thanks to the many friends, close family, and readers in Canada, Australia, the USA and beyond who've cheered me on, come to signings or launches, up me up for events or just let me rave about whatever idea has got me excited in that moment, and keep me from the edge of a nervous breakdown.

I am privileged and honoured to have you all.

ABOUT THE AUTHOR

Christian Baines is an awkward nerd turned slightly less awkward author. Raised on dark humour and powered by New Zealand wine, he is the author of six novels including gay paranormal series *The Arcadia Trust* and *My Cat's Guide to Online Dating*. Born in Australia, he now travels the world whenever possible, living and writing in Toronto, Canada between trips.

ALSO BY CHRISTIAN BAINES

THE ARCADIA TRUST *series:*
The Beast Without
The Orchard of Flesh
Sins of the Son
Tears in Time

Haunted Hearts:
Geist Fleisch

Other books:
Puppet Boy
Skin
My Cat's Guide to Online Dating

Praise for Christian Baines

"Baines' underworld is well devised, multi-layered, and dense with political and personal agendas—and it's frightening: so much so that I found myself looking over my shoulder more than once at night." FELICE PICANO, author of *Like People in History*

"Believable characters and rich settings pulled me into this world, and I didn't want to leave it. I was sorry to reach the end." GREG HERREN, author of the *Chanse MacLeod Mysteries* and the *Scotty Bradley Mysteries*

"A wickedly subversive wit." JEFFERY ROUND, author of *The Dan Sharp Mysteries*

"With excellent description and insights into what makes even the most supernatural figures human, Baines will have you staying up late to spend more time in his characters' unravelling world." A.J. DOLMAN, author of *Lost Enough*

"Just fantastic! I just couldn't put it down." SARINA, *Love Bytes Reviews*

"Christian Baines has an incredible talent for writing supernatural beings and making them absolutely credible." MELANIE MARSHALL, *Scattered Thoughts and Rogue Words*

"5 stars! ...a devastatingly good read!" CAMILLE, *Joyfully Jay*

"Christian Baines is a writer with a bold, original vision, a vision not beholden to the limits of conventional genre tropes. This is a writer who knows his own voice, and a writer to watch." MICHAEL ROWE, author of *Enter, Night*